They do it with Mirrors

Agatha Christie is known throughout the world as the Queen of Crime. Her books have sold over a billion copies in English with another billion in 100 foreign languages. She is the most widely published author of all time and in any language, outsold only by the Bible and Shakespeare. She is the author of 80 crime novels and short story collections, 19 plays, and six novels written under the name of Mary Westmacott.

Agatha Christie's first novel, *The Mysterious Affair at Styles*, was written towards the end of the First World War, in which she served as a VAD. In it she created Hercule Poirot, the little Belgian detective who was destined to become the most popular detective in crime fiction since Sherlock Holmes. It was eventually published by The Bodley Head in 1920.

In 1926, after averaging a book a year, Agatha Christie wrote her masterpiece. *The Murder of Roger Ackroyd* was the first of her books to be published by Collins and marked the beginning of an author-publisher relationship which lasted for 50 years and well over 70 books. *The Murder of Roger Ackroyd* was also the first of Agatha Christie's books to be dramatised – under the name *Alibi* – and to have a successful run in London's West End. *The Mousetrap*, her most famous play of all, opened in 1952 and is the longest-running play in history.

Agatha Christie was made a Dame in 1971. She died in 1976, since when a number of books have been published posthumously: the bestselling novel *Sleeping Murder* appeared later that year, followed by her autobiography and the short story collections *Miss Marple's Final Cases*, *Problem at Pollensa Bay* and *While the Light Lasts*. In 1998 *Black Coffee* was the first of her plays to be novelised by another author, Charles Osborne.

D1355436

The Agatha Christie Collection

The Man In The Brown Suit
The Secret of Chimneys
The Seven Dials Mystery
The Mysterious Mr Quin
The Sittaford Mystery
The Hound of Death
The Listerdale Mystery
Why Didn't They Ask Evans?
Parker Pyne Investigates
Murder Is Easy
And Then There Were None
Death Comes as the End
Sparkling Cyanide
Crooked House
They Came to Baghdad
Destination Unknown
Spider's Web *
The Unexpected Guest *
Ordeal by Innocence
The Pale Horse
Endless Night
Passenger To Frankfurt

Poirot
The Mysterious Affair at Styles
The Murder on the Links
Poirot Investigates
The Murder of Roger Ackroyd
The Big Four
The Mystery of the Blue Train
Black Coffee *
Peril at End House
Lord Edgware Dies
Murder on the Orient Express
Three-Act Tragedy
Death in the Clouds
The ABC Murders
Murder in Mesopotamia
Cards on the Table
Murder in the Mews
Dumb Witness
Death on the Nile
Appointment With Death
Hercule Poirot's Christmas
Sad Cypress
One, Two, Buckle My Shoe
Evil Under the Sun
Five Little Pigs
The Hollow
The Labours of Hercules

* novelised by Charles Osborne

Taken at the Flood
Mrs McGinty's Dead
After the Funeral
Hickory Dickory Dock
Dead Man's Folly
Cat Among the Pigeons
The Adventure of the Christmas Pudding
The Clocks
Third Girl
Hallowe'en Party
Elephants Can Remember
Poirot's Early Cases
Curtain: Poirot's Last Case

Marple
The Murder at the Vicarage
The Thirteen Problems
The Body in the Library
The Moving Finger
A Murder is Announced
They Do It With Mirrors
A Pocket Full of Rye
The 4.50 from Paddington
The Mirror Crack'd from Side to Side
A Caribbean Mystery
At Bertram's Hotel
Nemesis
Sleeping Murder
Miss Marple's Final Cases

Tommy & Tuppence
The Secret Adversary
Partners in Crime
N or M?
By the Pricking of My Thumbs
Postern of Fate

Published as Mary Westmacott
Giant's Bread
Unfinished Portrait
Absent in the Spring
The Rose and the Yew Tree
A Daughter's a Daughter
The Burden

Memoirs
An Autobiography
Come, Tell Me How You Live

Play Collections
The Mousetrap and Selected Plays
Witness for the Prosecution and
    Selected Plays

Agatha Christie

They do it
with Mirrors

TED SMART

This edition produced for The Book People Ltd,
Hall Wood Avenue,
Haydock, St Helens WA11 9UL

HarperCollins*Publishers*
77–85 Fulham Palace Road,
Hammersmith, London W6 8JB
www.harpercollins.co.uk

This *Agatha Christie Signature Edition* Published 2002
10 9 8 7 6 5 4 3 2 1

First Published in Great Britain by
Collins 1952

Copyright © Agatha Christie Mallowan 1952

ISBN 0 00 771692 3

Typeset by Palimpsest Book Production Limited,
Polmont, Stirlingshire

Printed and bound in Germany

To Mathew Prichard

Chapter 1

I

Mrs Van Rydock moved a little back from the mirror and sighed.

'Well, that'll have to do,' she murmured. 'Think it's all right, Jane?'

Miss Marple eyed the Lanvanelli creation appraisingly.

'It seems to me a very beautiful gown,' she said.

'The gown's all right,' said Mrs Van Rydock and sighed.

'Take if off, Stephanie,' she said.

The elderly maid with the grey hair and the small pinched mouth eased the gown carefully up over Mrs Van Rydock's upstretched arms.

Mrs Van Rydock stood in front of the glass in her peach satin slip. She was exquisitely corseted. Her still shapely legs were encased in fine nylon stockings. Her face, beneath a layer of cosmetics and constantly toned up by massage, appeared almost girlish at a slight distance. Her hair was less grey than tending to hydrangea blue and was perfectly set. It was practically impossible when looking at Mrs Van Rydock to imagine what she would be like in a natural state. Everything that money could do had been done for her – reinforced by diet, massage, and constant exercises.

Ruth Van Rydock looked humorously at her friend.

'Do you think most people would guess, Jane, that you and I are practically the same age?'

Miss Marple responded loyally.

'Not for a moment, I'm sure,' she said reassuringly. 'I'm afraid, you know, that *I* look every minute of *my* age!'

Miss Marple was white-haired, with a soft pink and white wrinkled face and innocent china blue eyes. She looked a very sweet old lady. Nobody would have called Mrs Van Rydock a sweet old lady.

'I guess you do, Jane,' said Mrs Van Rydock. She grinned suddenly, 'And so do I. Only not in the same way. "Wonderful how that old hag keeps her figure." That's what they say of me. But they know I'm an old hag all right! And, my God, do I feel like one!'

She dropped heavily on to the satin quilted chair.

'That's all right, Stephanie,' she said. 'You can go.'

Stephanie gathered up the dress and went out.

'Good old Stephanie,' said Ruth Van Rydock. 'She's

been with me for over thirty years now. She's the only woman who knows what I really look like! Jane, I want to talk to you.'

Miss Marple leant forward a little. Her face took on a receptive expression. She looked, somehow, an incongruous figure in the ornate bedroom of the expensive hotel suite. She was dressed in rather dowdy black, carried a large shopping bag and looked every inch a lady.

'I'm worried, Jane. About Carrie Louise.'

'Carrie Louise?' Miss Marple repeated the name musingly. The sound of it took her a long way back.

The pensionnat in Florence. Herself, the pink and white English girl from a Cathedral Close. The two Martin girls, Americans, exciting to the English girl because of their quaint ways of speech and their forthright manner and vitality. Ruth, tall, eager, on top of the world; Carrie Louise, small, dainty, wistful.

'When did you see her last, Jane?'

'Oh! not for many many years. It must be twenty-five at least. Of course we still send cards at Christmas.'

Such an odd thing, friendship! She, young Jane Marple, and the two Americans. Their ways diverging almost at once, and yet the old affection persisting; occasional letters, remembrances at Christmas. Strange that Ruth whose home – or rather homes – had been in America should be the sister whom she had seen

9

the more often of the two. No, perhaps not strange. Like most Americans of her class, Ruth had been cosmopolitan, every year or two she had come over to Europe, rushing from London to Paris, on to the Riviera, and back again, and always keen to snatch a few moments wherever she was with her old friends. There had been many meetings like this one. In Claridge's, or the Savoy, or the Berkeley, or the Dorchester. A *recherché* meal, affectionate reminiscences, and a hurried and affectionate goodbye. Ruth had never had time to visit St Mary Mead. Miss Marple had not, indeed, ever expected it. Everyone's life has a *tempo*. Ruth's was *presto* whereas Miss Marple's was content to be *adagio*.

So it was American Ruth whom she had seen most of, whereas Carrie Louise who lived in England, she had not now seen for over twenty years. Odd, but quite natural, because when one lives in the same country there is no need to arrange meetings with old friends. One assumes that, sooner or later, one will see them without contrivance. Only, if you move in different spheres, that does not happen. The paths of Jane Marple and Carrie Louise did not cross. It was as simple as that.

'Why are you worried about Carrie Louise, Ruth?' asked Miss Marple.

'In a way that's what worries me most! I just don't know.'

'She's not ill?'

'She's very delicate – always has been. I wouldn't say she'd been any worse than usual – considering that she's getting on just as we all are.'

'Unhappy?'

'Oh *no*.'

No, it wouldn't be that, thought Miss Marple. It would be difficult to imagine Carrie Louise unhappy – and yet there were times in her life when she must have been. Only – the picture did not come clearly. Bewildered – yes – incredulous – yes – but violent grief – no.

Mrs Van Rydock's words came appositely.

'Carrie Louise,' she said, 'has always lived right out of this world. She doesn't know what it's like. Maybe it's *that* that worries me.'

'Her circumstances,' began Miss Marple, then stopped, shaking her head. 'No,' she said.

'No, it's she herself,' said Ruth Van Rydock. 'Carrie Louise was always the one of us who had ideals. Of course it was the fashion when we were young to have ideals – we all had them, it was the proper thing for young girls. You were going to nurse lepers, Jane, and I was going to be a nun. One gets over all that nonsense. Marriage, I suppose one might say, knocks it out of one. Still, take it by and large, I haven't done badly out of marriage.'

11

Miss Marple thought that Ruth was expressing it mildly. Ruth had been married three times, each time to an extremely wealthy man, and the resultant divorces had increased her bank balance without in the least souring her disposition.

'Of course,' said Mrs Van Rydock, 'I've always been tough. Things don't get me down. I've not expected too much of life and certainly not expected too much of men – and I've done very well out of it – and no hard feelings. Tommy and I are still excellent friends, and Julius often asks me my opinion about the market.' Her face darkened. 'I believe that's what worries me about Carrie Louise – she's always had a tendency, you know, to marry *cranks*.'

'Cranks?'

'People with ideals. Carrie Louise was always a pushover for ideals. There she was, as pretty as they make them, just seventeen and listening with her eyes as big as saucers to old Gulbrandsen holding forth about his plans for the human race. Over fifty, and she married him, a widower with a family of grown-up children – all because of his philanthropic ideas. She used to sit listening to him spellbound. Just like Desdemona and Othello. Only fortunately there was no Iago about to mess things up – and anyway Gulbrandsen wasn't coloured. He was a Swede or a Norwegian or something.'

Miss Marple nodded thoughtfully. The name of Gulbrandsen had an international significance. A man who with shrewd business acumen and perfect honesty had built up a fortune so colossal that really philanthropy had been the only solution to the disposal of it. The name still held significance. The Gulbrandsen Trust, the Gulbrandsen Research Fellowships, the Gulbrandsen Administrative Almshouses, and best known of all the vast educational College for the sons of working men.

'She didn't marry him for his money, you know,' said Ruth, '*I* should have if I'd married him at all. But not Carrie Louise. I don't know what would have happened if he hadn't died when she was thirty-two. Thirty-two's a very nice age for a widow. She's got experience, but she's still adaptable.'

The spinster listening to her, nodded gently whilst her mind revived, tentatively, widows she had known in the village of St Mary Mead.

'I was really happiest about Carrie Louise when she was married to Johnnie Restarick. Of course *he* married her for her money – or if not exactly that, at any rate he wouldn't have married her if she hadn't had any. Johnnie was a selfish, pleasure-loving, lazy hound, but that's so much safer than a crank. All Johnnie wanted was to live soft. He wanted Carrie Louise to go to the best dressmakers and have yachts and cars and enjoy herself with him. That kind of man is so very *safe*. Give him comfort and luxury and he'll purr like a cat and be absolutely charming to you. I never took that scene designing and theatrical stuff of his very seriously. But Carrie Louise was thrilled by it – saw it all as Art with a capital A and really forced him back into those surroundings, and then that dreadful Yugoslavian woman got hold of him and just swept him off with her. He didn't really want to go. If Carrie Louise had waited and been sensible, he would have come back to her.'

'Did she care very much?' asked Miss Marple.

'That's the funny thing. I don't really believe she did. She was absolutely sweet about it all – but then she would be. She *is* sweet. Quite anxious to divorce him so that he and that creature could get married. And offering to give those two boys of his by his first marriage a home with her because it would be more settled for them. So there poor Johnnie was – he *had* to marry the woman and she led him an awful six months and then drove him over a precipice in a car in a fit of rage. They *said* it was an accident, but *I* think it was just temper!'

Mrs Van Rydock paused, took up a mirror and gazed at her face searchingly. She picked up her eyebrow tweezers and pulled out a hair.

'And what does Carrie Louise do next but marry

this man Lewis Serrocold. Another crank! Another man with ideals! Oh, I don't say he isn't devoted to her – I think he is – but he's bitten by that same bug of wanting to improve everybody's lives for them. And really, you know, nobody can do that but yourself.'

'I wonder,' said Miss Marple.

'Only, of course, there's a fashion in these things, just like there is in clothes. (My dear, have you seen what Christian Dior is trying to make us wear in the way of skirts?) Where was I? Oh yes, Fashion. Well there's a fashion in philanthropy too. It used to be education in Gulbrandsen's day. But that's out of date now. The State has stepped in. Everyone expects education as a matter of right – and doesn't think much of it when they get it! Juvenile Delinquency – that's what is the rage nowadays. All these young criminals and potential criminals. Everyone's mad about them. You should see Lewis Serrocold's eyes sparkle behind those thick glasses of his. Crazy with enthusiasm! One of those men of enormous will power who like living on a banana and a piece of toast and put all their energies into a Cause. And Carrie Louise eats it up – just as she always did. But I don't like it, Jane. They've had meetings of the Trustees and the whole place has been turned over to this new idea. It's a training establishment now for these juvenile criminals, complete with psychiatrists and psychologists and all

15

the rest of it. There Lewis and Carrie Louise are, living there, surrounded by these boys – who aren't perhaps quite normal. And the place stiff with occupational therapists and teachers and enthusiasts, half of *them* quite mad. Cranks, all the lot of them, and my little Carrie Louise in the middle of it all!'

She paused – and stared helplessly at Miss Marple.

Miss Marple said in a faintly puzzled voice:

'But you haven't told me yet, Ruth, what you are really afraid of.'

'I tell you, I don't *know*! And *that's* what worries me. I've just been down there – for a flying visit. And I felt all along that there was something wrong. In the atmosphere – in the house – I know I'm not mistaken. I'm sensitive to atmosphere, always have been. Did I ever tell you how I urged Julius to sell out of Amalgamated Cereals before the crash came? And wasn't I right? Yes, something is *wrong* down there. But I don't know why or what – if it's these dreadful young jailbirds – or if it's nearer home. I can't say what it is. There's Lewis just living for his ideas and not noticing anything else, and Carrie Louise, bless her, never seeing or hearing or thinking anything except what's a lovely sight, or a lovely sound, or a lovely thought. It's sweet but it isn't *practical*. There *is* such a thing as evil – and I want you, Jane, to go down there right away and find out just exactly what's the matter.'

'*Me?*' exclaimed Miss Marple. 'Why me?'

'Because you've got a nose for that sort of thing. You always had. You've always been a sweet innocent-looking creature, Jane, and all the time underneath nothing has ever surprised you, you always believe the worst.'

'The worst is so often true,' murmured Miss Marple.

'Why you have such a poor idea of human nature, I can't think – living in that sweet peaceful village of yours, so old world and pure.'

'You have never lived in a village, Ruth. The things that go on in a pure peaceful village would probably surprise you.'

'Oh I daresay. My point is that they don't surprise *you*. So you *will* go down to Stonygates and find out what's wrong, won't you?'

'But, Ruth dear, that would be a most difficult thing to do.'

'No, it wouldn't. I've thought it all out. If you won't be absolutely mad at me, I've prepared the ground already.'

Mrs Van Rydock paused, eyed Miss Marple rather uneasily, lighted a cigarette, and plunged rather nervously into explanation.

'You'll admit, I'm sure, that things have been difficult in this country since the war, for people with small fixed incomes – for people like you, that is to say, Jane.'

17

'Oh yes, indeed. But for the kindness, the really great kindness of my nephew Raymond, I don't know really where I should be.'

'Never mind your nephew,' said Mrs Van Rydock. 'Carrie Louise knows nothing about your nephew – or if she does, she knows him as a writer and has no idea that he's your nephew. The point, as I put it to Carrie Louise, is that it's just too bad about dear Jane. Really sometimes hardly enough to eat, and of course, far too proud ever to appeal to old friends. One couldn't, I said, suggest *money* – but a nice long rest in lovely surroundings, with an old friend and with plenty of nourishing food, and no cares or worries' – Ruth Van Rydock paused and then added defiantly, 'Now go on – be mad at me if you want to be.'

Miss Marple opened her china blue eyes in gentle surprise.

'But why should I be mad at you, Ruth? A very ingenious and plausible approach. I'm sure Carrie Louise responded.'

'She's writing to you. You'll find the letter when you get back. Honestly, Jane, you don't feel that I've taken an unpardonable liberty? You won't mind –'

She hesitated and Miss Marple put her thoughts deftly into words.

'Going to Stonygates as an object of charity – more or less under false pretences? Not in the least – if it is *necessary*. You think it is necessary – and I am inclined to agree with you.'

Mrs Van Rydock stared at her.

'But why? What have you heard?'

'I haven't heard anything. It's just your conviction. You're not a fanciful woman, Ruth.'

'No, but I haven't anything definite to go upon.'

'I remember,' said Miss Marple thoughtfully, 'one Sunday morning at church – it was the second Sunday in Advent – sitting behind Grace Lamble and feeling more and more worried about her. Quite sure, you know, that something was wrong – badly wrong – and yet being quite unable to say why. A most disturbing feeling and very very definite.'

'And was there something wrong?'

'Oh yes. Her father, the old Admiral, had been *very* peculiar for some time, and the very next day he went for her with the coal hammer, roaring out that she was Antichrist masquerading as his daughter. He nearly killed her. They took him away to the asylum and she eventually recovered after months in hospital – but it was a very near thing.'

'And you'd actually had a premonition that day in church?'

'I wouldn't call it a premonition. It was founded on *fact* – these things usually are, though one doesn't always recognise it at the time. She was wearing her

Agatha Christie

Sunday hat the wrong way round. Very significant, really, because Grace Lamble was a most precise woman, not at all vague or absent-minded – and the circumstances under which she would not notice which way her hat was put on to go to church were really extremely limited. Her father, you see, had thrown a marble paperweight at her and it had shattered the looking-glass. She had caught up her hat, put it on, and hurried out of the house. Anxious to keep up appearances and for the servants not to hear anything. She put down these actions, you see, to "dear Papa's Naval temper," she didn't realise that his mind was definitely unhinged. Though she ought to have realised it clearly enough. He was always complaining to her of being spied upon and of enemies – all the usual symptoms, in fact.'

Mrs Van Rydock gazed respectfully at her friend.

'Maybe, Jane,' she said, 'that St Mary Mead of yours isn't quite the idyllic retreat that I've always imagined it.'

'Human nature, dear, is very much the same everywhere. It is more difficult to observe it closely in a city, that is all.'

'And you'll go to Stonygates?'

'I'll go to Stonygates. A little unfair, perhaps, on my nephew Raymond. To let it be thought that he does not assist me, I mean. Still, the dear boy is in

Mexico for six months. And by that time it should all be over.'

'What should all be over?'

'Carrie Louise's invitation will hardly be for an indefinite stay. Three weeks, perhaps – a month. That should be ample.'

'For you to find out what is wrong?'

'For me to find out what is wrong.'

'My, Jane,' said Mrs Van Rydock, 'you've got a lot of confidence in yourself, haven't you?'

Miss Marple looked faintly reproachful.

'*You* have confidence in me, Ruth. Or so you say . . . I can only assure you that I shall endeavour to justify your confidence.'

Chapter 2

I

Before catching her train back to St Mary Mead (Wednesday special cheap day return), Miss Marple, in a precise and businesslike fashion, collected certain data.

'Carrie Louise and I have corresponded after a fashion, but it has largely been a matter of Christmas cards or calendars. It's just the facts I should like, Ruth dear – and also some idea as to whom exactly I shall encounter in the household at Stonygates.'

'Well, you know about Carrie Louise's marriage to Gulbrandsen. There were no children and Carrie Louise took that very much to heart. Gulbrandsen was a widower, and had three grown-up sons. Eventually they adopted a child. Pippa, they called her – a lovely little creature. She was just two years old when they got her.'

'Where did she come from? What was her background?'

'Really, now, Jane, I can't remember – if I ever heard, that is. An Adoption Society, maybe? Or some unwanted child that Gulbrandsen had heard about. Why? Do you think it's important?'

'Well, one always likes to know the background, so to speak. But please go on.'

'The next thing that happened was that Carrie Louise found that she was going to have a baby after all. I understand from doctors that that quite often happens.'

Miss Marple nodded.

'I believe so.'

'Anyway, it did happen, and in a funny kind of way, Carrie Louise was almost disconcerted, if you can understand what I mean. Earlier, of course, she'd have been wild with joy. As it was, she'd given such a devoted love to Pippa that she felt quite apologetic to Pippa for putting her nose out of joint, so to speak. And then Mildred, when she arrived, was really a very unattractive child. Took after the Gulbrandsens – who were solid and worthy – but definitely homely. Carrie Louise was always so anxious to make no difference between the adopted child and her own child that I think she rather tended to overindulge Pippa and pass over Mildred. Sometimes I think that Mildred resented it. However I didn't see them often. Pippa grew up a very beautiful girl and Mildred grew up a plain one.

Eric Gulbrandsen died when Mildred was fifteen and Pippa eighteen. At twenty Pippa married an Italian, the Marchese di San Severiano – oh, quite a genuine Marchese – not an adventurer, or anything like that. She was by way of being an heiress (naturally, or San Severiano wouldn't have married her – you know what Italians are!). Gulbrandsen left an equal sum in trust for both his own and his adopted daughter. Mildred married a Canon Strete – a nice man but given to colds in the head. About ten or fifteen years older than she was. Quite a happy marriage, I believe.

'He died a year ago and Mildred has come back to Stonygates to live with her mother. But that's getting on too fast, I've skipped a marriage or two. I'll go back to them. Pippa married her Italian. Carrie Louise was quite pleased about the marriage. Guido had beautiful manners and was very handsome, and he was a fine sportsman. A year later Pippa had a daughter and died in childbirth. It was a terrible tragedy and Guido San Severiano was very cut up. Carrie Louise went to and fro between Italy and England a good deal, and it was in Rome that she met Johnnie Restarick and married him. The Marchese married again and he was quite willing for his little daughter to be brought up in England by her exceedingly wealthy grandmother. So they all settled down at Stonygates, Johnnie Restarick and Carrie Louise, and Johnnie's two boys, Alexis and

Stephen (Johnnie's first wife was a Russian) and the baby Gina. Mildred married her Canon soon afterwards. Then came all this business of Johnnie and the Yugoslavian woman and the divorce. The boys still came to Stonygates for their holidays and were devoted to Carrie Louise, and then in 1938, I think it was, Carrie Louise married Lewis.'

Mrs Van Rydock paused for breath.

'You've not met Lewis?'

Miss Marple shook her head.

'No, I think I last saw Carrie Louise in 1928. She very sweetly took me to Covent Garden – to the Opera.'

'Oh yes. Well, Lewis was a very suitable person for her to marry. He was the head of a very celebrated firm of chartered accountants. I think he met her first over some questions of the finances of the Gulbrandsen Trust and the College. He was well off, just about her own age, and a man of absolutely upright life. But he *was* a crank. He was absolutely rabid on the subject of the redemption of young criminals.'

Ruth Van Rydock sighed.

'As I said just now, Jane, there are fashions in philanthropy. In Gulbrandsen's time it was education. Before that it was soup kitchens –'

Miss Marple nodded.

'Yes, indeed. Port wine jelly and calf's head broth taken to the sick. My mother used to do it.'

'That's right. Feeding the body gave way to feeding the mind. Everyone went mad on educating the lower classes. Well, that's passed. Soon, I expect, the fashionable thing to do will be not to educate your children, preserve their illiteracy carefully until they're eighteen. Anyway the Gulbrandsen Trust and Education Fund was in some difficulties because the State was taking over its functions. Then Lewis came along with his passionate enthusiasm about constructive training for juvenile delinquents. His attention had been drawn to the subject first in the course of his profession – auditing accounts where ingenious young men had perpetrated frauds. He was more and more convinced that juvenile delinquents were not subnormal – that they had excellent brains and abilities and only needed right direction.'

'There is something in that,' said Miss Marple. 'But it is not entirely true. I remember –'

She broke off and glanced at her watch.

'Oh dear – I mustn't miss the 6.30.'

Ruth Van Rydock said urgently:

'And you will go to Stonygates?'

Gathering up her shopping bag and her umbrella Miss Marple said:

'If Carrie Louise asks me –'

'She will ask you. You'll go? Promise, Jane?'

Jane Marple promised.

Chapter 3

I

Miss Marple got out of the train at Market Kindle station. A kindly fellow passenger handed out her suitcase after her, and Miss Marple, clutching a string bag, a faded leather handbag and some miscellaneous wraps, uttered appreciative twitters of thanks.

'So kind of you, I'm sure . . . So difficult nowadays – not many porters. I get so flustered when I travel.'

The twitters were drowned by the booming noise of the station announcer saying loudly but indistinctly that the 3.18 was standing at Platform 1, and was about to proceed to various unidentifiable stations.

Market Kindle was a large empty windswept station with hardly any passengers or railway staff to be seen on it. Its claim to distinction lay in having six platforms and a bay where a very small train of one carriage was puffing importantly.

Miss Marple, rather more shabbily dressed than was

her custom (so lucky that she hadn't given away the old speckledy), was peering around her uncertainly when a young man came up to her.

'Miss Marple?' he said. His voice had an unexpectedly dramatic quality about it, as though the utterance of her name were the first words of a part he was playing in amateur theatricals. 'I've come to meet you – from Stonygates.'

Miss Marple looked gratefully at him, a charming helpless-looking old lady with, if he had chanced to notice it, very shrewd blue eyes. The personality of the young man did not quite match his voice. It was less important, one might almost say insignificant. His eyelids had a trick of fluttering nervously.

'Oh thank you,' said Miss Marple. 'There's just this suitcase.'

She noticed that the young man did not pick up her suitcase himself. He flipped a finger at a porter who was trundling some packing cases past on a trolley.

'Bring it out, please,' he said, and added importantly, 'for Stonygates.'

The porter said cheerfully:

'Rightyho. Shan't be long.'

Miss Marple fancied that her new acquaintance was not too pleased about this. It was as if Buckingham Palace had been dismissed as no more important than 3 Laburnum Road.

He said, 'The railways get more impossible every day!'

Guiding Miss Marple towards the exit, he said: 'I'm Edgar Lawson. Mrs Serrocold asked me to meet you. I help Mr Serrocold in his work.'

There was again the faint insinuation that a busy and important man had, very charmingly, put important affairs on one side out of chivalry to his employer's wife.

And again the impression was not wholly convincing – it had a theatrical flavour.

Miss Marple began to wonder about Edgar Lawson.

They came out of the station and Edgar guided the old lady to where a rather elderly Ford V. 8 was standing.

He was just saying 'Will you come in front with me, or would you prefer the back?' when there was a diversion.

A new gleaming two-seater Rolls Bentley came purring into the station yard and drew up in front of the Ford. A very beautiful young woman jumped out of it and came across to them. The fact that she wore dirty corduroy slacks and a simple shirt open at the neck seemed somehow to enhance the fact that she was not only beautiful but expensive.

'There you are, Edgar. I thought I wouldn't make it in time. I see you've got Miss Marple. I came to meet her.' She smiled dazzlingly at Miss Marple, showing a row of lovely teeth in a sunburnt southern face. 'I'm Gina,' she said. 'Carrie Louise's granddaughter. What was your journey like? Simply foul? What a nice string bag. I *love* string bags. I'll take it and the coats and then you can get in better.'

Edgar's face flushed. He protested.

'Look here, Gina, I came to meet Miss Marple. It was all arranged . . .'

Again the teeth flashed in that wide lazy smile.

'Oh I know, Edgar, but I suddenly thought it would be nice if I came along. I'll take her with me and you can wait and bring her cases up.'

She slammed the door on Miss Marple, ran round to the other side, jumped in the driving seat, and they purred swiftly out of the station.

Looking back, Miss Marple noticed Edgar Lawson's face.

'I don't think, my dear,' she said, 'that Mr Lawson is very pleased.'

Gina laughed.

'Edgar's a frightful idiot,' she said. 'Always so pompous about things. You'd really think he *mattered*!'

Miss Marple asked, 'Doesn't he matter?'

'Edgar?' There was an unconscious note of cruelty in Gina's scornful laugh. 'Oh, he's bats anyway.'

'Bats?'

'They're all bats at Stonygates,' said Gina. 'I don't mean Lewis and Grandam and me and the boys – and not Miss Bellever, of course. But the others. Sometimes I feel *I*'m going a bit bats myself living there. Even Aunt Mildred goes out on walks and mutters to herself all the time – and you don't expect a Canon's widow to do that, do you?'

They swung out of the station approach and accelerated up the smooth surfaced empty road. Gina shot a swift sideways glance at her companion.

'You were at school with Grandam, weren't you? It seems so queer.'

Miss Marple knew perfectly what she meant. To youth it seems very odd to think that age was once young and pigtailed and struggled with decimals and English literature.

'It must,' said Gina with awe in her voice, and obviously not meaning to be rude, 'have been a *very* long time ago.'

'Yes, indeed,' said Miss Marple. 'You feel that more with me than you do with your grandmother, I expect?'

Gina nodded. 'It's cute of you saying that. Grandam, you know, gives one a curiously ageless feeling.'

'It is a long time since I've seen her. I wonder if I shall find her much changed.'

'Her hair's grey, of course,' said Gina vaguely. 'And she walks with a stick because of her arthritis. It's got much worse lately. I suppose that –' she broke off, and then asked: 'Have you been to Stonygates before?'

'No, never. I've heard a great deal about it, of course.'

'It's pretty ghastly, really,' said Gina cheerfully. 'A sort of Gothic monstrosity. What Steve calls Best Victorian Lavatory period. But it's fun, too, in a way. Only of course everything's madly earnest, and you tumble over psychiatrists everywhere underfoot. Enjoying themselves madly. Rather like Scout-masters, only worse. The young criminals are rather pets, some of them. One showed me how to diddle locks with a bit of wire and one angelic-faced boy gave me a lot of points about coshing people.'

Miss Marple considered this information thoughtfully.

'It's the thugs I like best,' said Gina. 'I don't fancy the queers so much. Of course Lewis and Dr Maverick think they're *all* queer – I mean they think it's repressed desires and disordered home life and their mothers getting off with soldiers and all that. I don't really see it myself because some people have had awful home lives and yet have managed to turn out quite all right.'

'I'm sure it is all a very difficult problem,' said Miss Marple.

Gina laughed, again showing her magnificent teeth.

'It doesn't worry me much. I suppose some people have these sort of urges to make the world a better place. Lewis is quite dippy about it all – he's going to Aberdeen next week because there's a case coming up in the police court – a boy with five previous convictions.'

'The young man who met me at the station? Mr Lawson. He helps Mr Serrocold, he told me. Is he his secretary?'

'Oh Edgar hasn't brains enough to be a secretary. He's a *case*, really. He used to stay at hotels and pretend he was a V.C. or a fighter pilot and borrow money and then do a flit. I think he's just a rotter. But Lewis goes through a routine with them all. Makes them feel one of the family and gives them jobs to do and all that to encourage their sense of responsibility. I daresay we shall be murdered by one of them one of these days.' Gina laughed merrily.

Miss Marple did not laugh.

They turned in through some imposing gates where a Commissionaire was standing on duty in a military manner and drove up a drive flanked with rhododendrons. The drive was badly kept and the grounds seemed neglected.

Interpreting her companion's glance, Gina said, 'No gardeners during the war, and since we haven't bothered. But it does look rather terrible.'

35

Agatha Christie

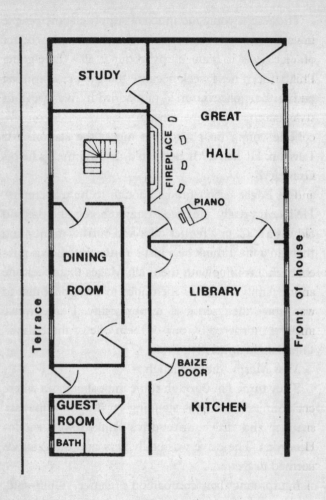

Plan of Stonygates

They came round a curve and Stonygates appeared in its full glory. It was, as Gina had said, a vast edifice of Victorian Gothic – a kind of temple to Plutocracy. Philanthropy had added to it in various wings and outbuildings which, while not positively dissimilar in style, had robbed the structure as a whole of any cohesion or purpose.

'Hideous, isn't it?' said Gina affectionately. 'There's Grandam on the terrace. I'll stop here and you can go and meet her.'

Miss Marple advanced along the terrace towards her old friend.

From a distance, the slim little figure looked curiously girlish in spite of the stick on which she leaned and her slow and obviously rather painful progress. It was as though a young girl was giving an exaggerated imitation of old age.

'Jane,' said Mrs Serrocold.

'Dear Carrie Louise.'

Yes, unmistakably Carrie Louise. Strangely unchanged, strangely youthful still, although, unlike her sister, she used no cosmetics or artificial aids to youth. Her hair was grey, but it had always been of a silvery fairness and the colour had changed very little. Her skin had still a rose leaf pink and white appearance, though now it was a crumpled rose leaf. Her eyes had still their starry innocent glance. She had the slender

37

youthful figure of a girl and her head kept its eager birdlike tilt.

'I do blame myself,' said Carrie Louise in her sweet voice, 'for letting it be so long. *Years* since I saw you, Jane dear. It's just lovely that you've come at last to pay us a visit here.'

From the end of the terrace Gina called:

'You ought to come in, Grandam. It's getting cold – and Jolly will be furious.'

Carrie Louise gave her little silvery laugh.

'They all fuss about me so,' she said. 'They rub it in that I'm an old woman.'

'And you don't feel like one.'

'No, I don't, Jane. In spite of all my aches and pains and I've got plenty. Inside I go on feeling just a chit like Gina. Perhaps everyone does. The glass shows them how old they are and they just don't believe it. It seems only a few months ago that we were at Florence. Do you remember Fraulein Schweich and her boots?'

The two elderly women laughed together at events that had happened nearly half a century ago.

They walked together to a side door. In the doorway a gaunt elderly lady met them. She had an arrogant nose, a short haircut and wore stout well-cut tweeds.

She said fiercely:

'It's absolutely crazy of you, Cara, to stay out so late.

You're absolutely incapable of taking care of yourself. What will Mr Serrocold say?'

'Don't scold me, Jolly,' said Carrie Louise pleadingly.

She introduced Miss Bellever to Miss Marple.

'This is Miss Bellever, who is simply everything to me. Nurse, dragon, watchdog, secretary, housekeeper and very faithful friend.'

Juliet Bellever sniffed, and the end of her big nose turned rather pink, a sign of emotion.

'I do what I can,' she said gruffly. 'This is a crazy household. You simply can't arrange any kind of planned routine.'

'Darling Jolly, of course you can't. I wonder why you ever try. Where are you putting Miss Marple?'

'In the Blue Room. Shall I take her up?' asked Miss Bellever.

'Yes, please do, Jolly. And then bring her down to tea. It's in the library today, I think.'

The Blue Room had heavy curtains of a rich faded blue brocade that must have been, Miss Marple thought, about fifty years old. The furniture was mahogany, big and solid, and the bed was a vast mahogany fourposter. Miss Bellever opened a door into a connecting bathroom. This was unexpectedly modern, orchid in colouring and with much dazzling chromium.

She observed grimly:

'John Restarick had ten bathrooms put into the house

when he married Cara. The plumbing is about the only thing that's ever been modernized. He wouldn't hear of the rest being altered – said the whole place was a perfect Period Piece. Did you ever know him at all?'

'No, I never met him. Mrs Serrocold and I have met very seldom though we have always corresponded.'

'He was an agreeable fellow,' said Miss Bellever. 'No good, of course! A complete rotter. But pleasant to have about the house. Great charm. Women liked him far too much. That was his undoing in the end. Not really Cara's type.'

She added with a brusque resumption of her practical manner:

'The housemaid will unpack for you. Do you want a wash before tea?'

Receiving an affirmative answer, she said that Miss Marple would find her waiting at the top of the stairs.

Miss Marple went into the bathroom and washed her hands and dried them a little nervously on a very beautiful orchid-coloured face towel. Then she removed her hat and patted her soft white hair into place.

Opening her door, she found Miss Bellever waiting for her, and was conducted down the big gloomy staircase and across a vast dark hall and into a room where bookshelves went up to the ceiling and a big window looked out over an artificial lake.

Carrie Louise was standing by the window and Miss Marple joined her.

'What a very imposing house this is,' said Miss Marple. 'I feel quite lost in it.'

'Yes, I know. It's ridiculous, really. It was built by a prosperous iron master – or something of that kind. He went bankrupt not long after. I don't wonder really. There were about fourteen living-rooms – all enormous. I've never seen what people *can* want with more than one sitting-room. And all those huge bedrooms. Such a lot of unnecessary space. Mine is terribly overpowering – and quite a long way to walk from the bed to the dressing table. And great heavy dark crimson curtains.'

'You haven't had it modernized and redecorated?'

Carrie Louise looked vaguely surprised.

'No. On the whole it's very much as it was when I first lived here with Eric. It's been repainted, of course, but they always do it the same colour. Those things don't really matter, do they? I mean I shouldn't have felt justified in spending a lot of money on that kind of thing when there are so many things that are so much more important.'

'Have there been no changes at all in the house?'

'Oh – yes – heaps of them. We've just kept a kind of block in the middle of the house as it was – the Great Hall and the rooms off and over. They're the best ones

41

and Johnnie – my second husband – was lyrical over them and said they should never be touched or altered – and of course he was an artist and a designer and he knew about these things. But the East and West wings have been completely remodelled. All the rooms partitioned off and divided up, so that we have offices, and bedrooms for the teaching staff, and all that. The boys are all in the College building – you can see it from here.'

Miss Marple looked out towards where large red brick buildings showed through a belt of sheltered trees. Then her eyes fell on something nearer at hand, and she smiled a little.

'What a very beautiful girl Gina is,' she said.

Carrie Louise's face lit up.

'Yes, isn't she?' she said softly. 'It's so lovely to have her back here again. I sent her to America at the beginning of the war – to Ruth. Did Ruth talk about her at all?'

'No. At least she did just mention her.'

Carrie Louise sighed.

'Poor Ruth! She was frightfully upset over Gina's marriage. But I've told her again and again that I don't blame her in the least. Ruth doesn't realize, as I do, that the old barriers and class shibboleths are gone – or at any rate are going.

'Gina was doing her war work – and she met this

young man. He was a Marine and had a very good war record. And a week later they were married. It was all far too quick, of course, no time to find out if they were really suited to each other – but that's the way of things nowadays. Young people belong to their generation. We may think they're unwise in many of their doings, but we have to accept their decisions. Ruth, though, was terribly upset.'

'She didn't consider the young man suitable?'

'She kept saying that one didn't know anything about him. He came from the Middle West and he hadn't any money – and naturally no profession. There are hundreds of boys like that everywhere – but it wasn't Ruth's idea of what was right for Gina. However, the thing was done. I was so glad when Gina accepted my invitation to come over here with her husband. There's so much going on here – jobs of every kind, and if Walter wants to specialize in medicine or get a degree or anything he could do it in this country. After all, this is Gina's home. It's delightful to have her back, to have someone so warm and gay and alive in the house.'

Miss Marple nodded and looked out of the window again at the two young people standing near the lake.

'They're a remarkably handsome couple, too,' she said. 'I don't wonder Gina fell in love with him!'

'Oh, but that – that isn't Wally.' There was, quite

Agatha Christie

suddenly, a touch of embarrassment, or restraint, in Mrs Serrocold's voice. 'That's Steve – the younger of Johnnie Restarick's two boys. When Johnnie – when he went away, he'd no place for the boys in the holidays, so I always had them here. They look on this as their home. And Steve's here permanently now. He runs our dramatic branch. We have a theatre, you know, and plays – we encourage all the artistic instincts. Lewis says that so much of this juvenile crime is due to exhibitionism, most of the boys have had such a thwarted unhappy home life, and these hold-ups and burglaries make them feel heroes. We urge them to write their own plays and act in them and design and paint their own scenery. Steve is in charge of the theatre. He's so keen and enthusiastic. It's wonderful what life he's put into the whole thing.'

'I see,' said Miss Marple slowly.

Her long-distance sight was good (as many of her neighbours knew to their cost in the village of St Mary Mead) and she saw very clearly the dark handsome face of Stephen Restarick as he stood facing Gina, talking eagerly. Gina's face she could not see, since the girl had her back to them, but there was no mistaking the expression in Stephen Restarick's face.

'It isn't any business of mine,' said Miss Marple, 'but I suppose you realize, Carrie Louise, that he's in love with her.'

'Oh no –' Carrie Louise looked troubled. 'Oh no, I do hope not.'

'You were always up in the clouds, Carrie Louise. There's not the least doubt about it.'

Chapter 4

I

Before Mrs Serrocold could say anything, her husband came in from the hall carrying some open letters in his hand.

Lewis Serrocold was a short man, not particularly impressive in appearance, but with a personality that immediately marked him out. Ruth had once said of him that he was more like a dynamo than a human being. He usually concentrated entirely on what was immediately occupying his attention and paid no attention to the objects or persons who were surrounding them.

'A bad blow, dearest,' he said. 'That boy, Jackie Flint. Back at his tricks again. And I really did think he meant to go straight this time if he got a proper chance. He was most earnest about it. You know we found he'd always been keen on railways – and both Maverick and I thought that if he got a job on the railways he'd stick to it and make good. But it's the same story. Petty thieving from the parcels office. Not even stuff he could want or sell. That shows that it *must* be psychological. We haven't really got to the root of the trouble. But I'm not giving up.'

'Lewis – this is my old friend, Jane Marple.'

'Oh how d'you do,' said Mr Serrocold absently. 'So glad – they'll prosecute, of course. A nice lad, too, not too many brains, but a really nice boy. Unspeakable home he came from. I –'

He suddenly broke off, and the dynamo was switched on to the guest.

'Why, Miss Marple, I'm so delighted you've come to stay with us for a while. It will make such a great difference to Caroline to have a friend of old days with whom she can exchange memories. She has in many ways a grim time here – so much sadness in the stories of these poor children. We do hope you'll stay with us a very long time.'

Miss Marple felt the magnetism and realized how attractive it would have been to her friend. That Lewis Serrocold was a man who would always put causes before people she did not doubt for a moment. It might have irritated some women, but not Carrie Louise.

Lewis Serrocold sorted out another letter.

'At any rate we've *some* good news. This is from the Wiltshire and Somerset Bank. Young Morris is doing extremely well. They're thoroughly satisfied with him and in fact are promoting him next month. I always knew that all he needed was responsibility – that, and a thorough grasp of the handling of money and what it means.'

He turned to Miss Marple.

'Half these boys don't *know* what money is. It represents to them going to the pictures or to the dogs, or buying cigarettes – and they're clever with figures and find it exciting to juggle them round. Well, I believe in – what shall I say? – rubbing their noses in the stuff – train them in accountancy, in figures – show them the whole inner romance of money, so to speak. Give them skill and then responsibility – let them handle it officially. Our greatest successes have been that way – only two out of thirty-eight have let us down. One's head cashier in a firm of druggists – a really responsible position –'

He broke off to say: 'Tea's in, dearest,' to his wife.

'I thought we were having it here. I told Jolly.'

'No, it's in the Hall. The others are there.'

'I thought they were all going to be out.'

Carrie Louise linked her arm through Miss Marple's and they went into the Great Hall. Tea seemed a rather incongruous meal in its surroundings. The tea things were piled haphazard on a tray – white utility cups mixed with the remnants of what had been

49

Rockingham and Spode tea services. There was a loaf of bread, two pots of jam, and some cheap and unwholesome-looking cakes.

A plump middle-aged woman with grey hair sat behind the tea table and Mrs Serrocold said:

'This is Mildred, Jane. My daughter Mildred. You haven't seen her since she was a tiny girl.'

Mildred Strete was the person most in tune with the house that Miss Marple had so far seen. She looked prosperous and dignified. She had married late in her thirties a Canon of the Church of England and was now a widow. She looked exactly like a Canon's widow, respectable and slightly dull. She was a plain woman with a large unexpressive face and dull eyes. She had been, Miss Marple reflected, a very plain little girl.

'And this is Wally Hudd – Gina's husband.'

Wally was a big young man with hair brushed up on his head and a sulky expression. He nodded awkwardly and went on cramming cake into his mouth.

Presently Gina came in with Stephen Restarick. They were both very animated.

'Gina's got a wonderful idea for that backcloth,' said Stephen. 'You know, Gina, you've got a very definite flair for theatrical designing.'

Gina laughed and looked pleased. Edgar Lawson came in and sat down by Lewis Serrocold. When Gina spoke to him, he made a pretence of not answering.

Miss Marple found it all a little bewildering and was glad to go to her room and lie down after tea.

There were more people still at dinner, a young Dr Maverick who was either a psychiatrist or a psychologist – Miss Marple was rather hazy about the difference – and whose conversation, dealing almost entirely with the jargon of his trade, was practically unintelligible to her. There were also two spectacled young men who held posts on the teaching side, and a Mr Baumgarten, who was an occupational therapist, and three intensely bashful youths who were doing their 'house guest' week. One of them, a fairhaired lad with very blue eyes was, Gina informed her in a whisper, the expert with the 'cosh'.

The meal was not a particularly appetizing one. It was indifferently cooked and indifferently served. A variety of costumes were worn. Miss Bellever wore a high black dress, Mildred Strete wore evening dress and a woollen cardigan over it. Carrie Louise had on a short dress of grey wool – Gina was resplendent in a kind of peasant get up. Wally had not changed, nor had Stephen Restarick, Edgar Lawson had on a neat dark blue suit. Lewis Serrocold wore the conventional dinner jacket. He ate very little and hardly seemed to notice what was on his plate.

After dinner Lewis Serrocold and Dr Maverick went away to the latter's office. The occupational therapist and the schoolmasters went away to some lair of their own. The three 'cases' went back to the college. Gina and Stephen went to the theatre to discuss Gina's idea for a set. Mildred knitted an indeterminate garment and Miss Bellever darned socks. Wally sat in a chair gently tilted backwards and stared into space. Carrie Louise and Miss Marple talked about old days. The conversation seemed strangely unreal.

Edgar Lawson alone seemed unable to find a niche. He sat down and then got up restlessly.

'I wonder if I ought to go to Mr Serrocold,' he said rather loudly. 'He may need me.'

Carrie Louise said gently, 'Oh I don't think so. He was going to talk over one or two points with Dr Maverick this evening.'

'Then I certainly won't butt in! I shouldn't dream of going where I wasn't wanted. I've already wasted time today going down to the station when Mrs Hudd meant to go herself.'

'She ought to have told you,' said Carrie Louise. 'But I think she just decided at the last moment.'

'You do realize, Mrs Serrocold, that she made me look a complete fool! A complete fool!'

'No, no,' said Carrie Louise, smiling. 'You mustn't have these ideas.'

'I know I'm not needed or wanted . . . I'm perfectly aware of *that*. If things had been different – if I'd had my proper place in life it would be very different. Very different indeed. It's no fault of mine that I haven't got my proper place in life.'

'Now, Edgar,' said Carrie Louise. 'Don't work yourself up about nothing. Jane thinks it was very kind of you to meet her. Gina always has these sudden impulses – she didn't mean to upset you.'

'Oh yes, she did. It was done on purpose – to humiliate me –'

'Oh Edgar –'

'You don't know half of what's going on, Mrs Serrocold. Well, I won't say any more now except goodnight.'

Edgar went out, shutting the door with a slam behind him.

Miss Bellever snorted:

'Atrocious manners.'

'He's so sensitive,' said Carrie Louise vaguely.

Mildred Strete clicked her needles and said sharply:

'He really is a most odious young man. You shouldn't put up with such behaviour, Mother.'

'Lewis says he can't help it.'

Mildred said sharply:

'Everyone can help behaving rudely. Of course I blame Gina very much. She's so completely scatterbrained in everything she undertakes. She does nothing but make trouble. One day she encourages the young man and the next day she snubs him. What can you expect?'

Wally Hudd spoke for the first time that evening.

He said:

'That guy's crackers. That's all there is to it! Crackers!'

II

In her bedroom that night Miss Marple tried to review the pattern of Stonygates, but it was as yet too confused. There were currents and cross-currents here – but whether they could account for Ruth Van Rydock's uneasiness it was impossible to tell. It did not seem to Miss Marple that Carrie Louise was affected in any way by what was going on round her. Stephen was in love with Gina. Gina might or might not be in love with Stephen. Walter Hudd was clearly not enjoying himself. These were incidents that might and did occur in all places and at most times. There was, unfortunately, nothing exceptional about them. They ended in the divorce court and everybody hopefully started again – when fresh tangles were created. Mildred Strete was clearly jealous of Gina and disliked her. That, Miss Marple thought, was very natural.

She thought over what Ruth Van Rydock had told her. Carrie Louise's disappointment at not having a child – the adoption of little Pippa – and then the discovery that, after all, a child was on the way.

'Often happens like that,' Miss Marple's doctor had told her. Relief of tension, maybe, and then Nature can do its work.

He had added that it was usually hard lines on the adopted child.

But that had not been so in this case. Both Gulbrandsen and his wife had adored little Pippa. She had made her place too firmly in their hearts to be lightly set aside. Gulbrandsen was already a father. Paternity meant nothing new to him. Carrie Louise's maternal yearnings had been assuaged by Pippa. Her pregnancy had been uncomfortable and the actual birth difficult and prolonged. Possibly Carrie Louise, who had never cared for reality, did not enjoy her first brush with it.

There remained two little girls growing up, one pretty and amusing, the other plain and dull. Which again, Miss Marple thought, was quite natural. For when people adopt a baby girl, they choose a pretty one. And though Mildred might have been lucky and taken after the Martins who had produced handsome Ruth and dainty Carrie Louise, Nature elected that she should take after the Gulbrandsens, who were large and stolid and uncompromisingly plain.

Moreover, Carrie Louise was determined that the adopted child should never feel her position, and in making sure of this she was over-indulgent to Pippa and sometimes less than fair to Mildred.

Pippa had married and gone away to Italy, and Mildred for a time had been the only daughter of the house. But then Pippa had died and Carrie Louise had brought Pippa's baby back to Stonygates, and once more Mildred had been out of it. There had been the new marriage – the Restarick boys. In 1934 Mildred had married Canon Strete, a scholarly antiquarian about fifteen years her senior and had gone away to live in the South of England. Presumably she had been happy – but one did not really know. There had been no children. And now here she was, back again in the same house where she had been brought up. And once again, Miss Marple thought, not particularly happy in it.

Gina, Stephen, Wally, Mildred, Miss Bellever who liked an ordered routine and was unable to enforce it. Lewis Serrocold who was clearly blissfully and whole-heartedly happy; an idealist able to translate his ideals into practical measures. In none of these personalities did Miss Marple find what Ruth's words had led her to believe she might find. Carrie Louise seemed secure, remote at the heart of the whirlpool – as she had been all her life. What then, in that atmosphere, had Ruth felt to be wrong . . . ? Did she, Jane Marple, feel it also?

What of the outer personalities of the whirlpool – the occupational therapists, the schoolmasters, earnest, harmless young men, confident young Dr Maverick, the three pink-faced innocent-eyed young delinquents – Edgar Lawson . . .

And here, just before she fell asleep, Miss Marple's thoughts stopped and revolved speculatively round the figure of Edgar Lawson. Edgar Lawson reminded her of someone or something. There *was* something a little wrong about Edgar Lawson – perhaps more than a little. Edgar Lawson was maladjusted – that was the phrase, wasn't it? But surely that didn't, and couldn't touch Carrie Louise?'

Mentally, Miss Marple shook her head.

What worried her was something more than that.

Chapter 5

I

Gently eluding her hostess the next morning, Miss Marple went out into the gardens. Their condition distressed her. They had once been an ambitiously set out achievement. Clumps of rhododendrons, smooth slopes of lawns, massed borders of herbaceous plants, clipped boxhedges surrounding a formal rose garden. Now all was largely derelict, the lawns raggedly mown, the borders full of weeds with tangled flowers struggling through them, the paths moss-covered and neglected. The kitchen gardens, on the other hand, enclosed by red brick walls, were prosperous and well stocked. That, presumably, was because they had a utility value. So, also, a large portion of what had once been lawn and flower garden, was now fenced off and laid out in tennis courts and a bowling green.

Surveying the herbaceous border, Miss Marple

clicked her tongue vexedly and pulled up a flourishing plant of groundsel.

As she stood with it in her hand, Edgar Lawson came into view. Seeing Miss Marple, he stopped and hesitated. Miss Marple had no mind to let him escape. She called him briskly. When he came, she asked him if he knew where any gardening tools were kept.

Edgar said vaguely that there was a gardener somewhere who would know.

'It's such a pity to see this border so neglected,' twittered Miss Marple. 'I'm so fond of gardens.' And since it was not her intention that Edgar should go in search of any necessary implement she went on quickly:

'It's about all an old and useless woman can find to do. Now I don't suppose *you* ever bother your head about gardens, Mr Lawson. You have so much real and important work to do. Being in a responsible position here, with Mr Serrocold. You must find it all most interesting.'

He answered quickly, almost eagerly:

'Yes – yes – it is interesting.'

'And you must be of the greatest assistance to Mr Serrocold.'

His face darkened.

'I don't know. I can't be sure. It's what's *behind* it all –'

He broke off. Miss Marple watched him thought-fully. A pathetic undersized young man in a neat dark suit. A young man that few people would look at twice, or remember if they did look . . .

There was a garden seat nearby and Miss Marple drifted towards it and sat. Edgar stood frowning in front of her.

'I'm sure,' said Miss Marple brightly, 'that Mr Serrocold relies on you a *great* deal.'

'I don't know,' said Edgar. 'I really don't know.' He frowned and almost absently sat down beside her. 'I'm in a very difficult position.'

'Of course,' said Miss Marple.

The young man Edgar sat staring in front of him.

'This is all highly confidential,' he said suddenly.

'Of course,' said Miss Marple.

'If I had my rights –'

'Yes?'

'I might as well tell you . . . You won't let it go any further I'm sure?'

'Oh no.' She noticed he did not wait for her disclaimer.

'My father – actually, my father is a very important man.'

This time there was no need to say anything. She had only to listen.

'Nobody knows except Mr Serrocold. You see, it

61

might prejudice my father's position if the story got out.' He turned to her. He smiled. A sad dignified smile. 'You see, *I'm Winston Churchill's son.*'

'Oh,' said Miss Marple. 'I *see.*'

And she did see. She remembered a rather sad story in St Mary Mead – and the way it had gone.

Edgar Lawson went on, and what he said had the familiarity of a stage scene.

'There were reasons. My mother wasn't free. Her own husband was in an asylum – there could be no divorce – no question of marriage. I don't really blame them. At least, I think I don't . . . He's done, always, everything he could. Discreetly, of course. And that's where the trouble has arisen. He's got enemies – and they're against me, too. They've managed to keep us apart. They watch me. Wherever I go, they spy on me. And they make things go wrong for me.'

Miss Marple shook her head.

'Dear, dear,' she said.

'In London I was studying to be a doctor. They tampered with my exams – they altered the answers. They *wanted* me to fail. They followed me about the streets. They told things about me to my landlady. They hound me wherever I go.'

'Oh, but you can't be sure of that,' said Miss Marple soothingly.

'I tell you I *know*! Oh they're very cunning. I never

get a glimpse of them or find out who they are. But I shall find out . . . Mr Serrocold took me away from London and brought me down here. He was kind – very kind. But even here, you know, I'm not *safe*. They're here too. Working against me. Making the others dislike me. Mr Serrocold says that isn't true – but Mr Serrocold doesn't know. Or else – I wonder – sometimes I've thought –'

He broke off. He got up.

'This is all confidential,' he said. 'You do understand that, don't you? But if you notice anyone *following* me – *spying*, I mean – you might let me know *who it is!*'

He went away, then – neat, pathetic, insignificant. Miss Marple watched him and wondered . . .

A voice spoke.

'Nuts,' it said. 'Just nuts.'

Walter Hudd was standing beside her. His hands were thrust deep in his pockets and he was frowning as he stared after Edgar's retreating figure.

'What kind of a joint is this, anyway?' he said. 'They're all bughouse, the whole lot of them.'

Miss Marple said nothing and Walter went on:

'That Edgar guy – what do you make of him? Says his father's really Lord Montgomery. Doesn't seem likely to me. Not *Monty*! Not from all I've heard about him.'

'No,' said Miss Marple. 'It doesn't seem very likely.'

'He told Gina something quite different – some bunk about being really the heir to the Russian throne – said he was some Grand Duke's son or other. Hell, doesn't the chap know who his father really was?'

'I should imagine not,' said Miss Marple. 'That is probably just the trouble.'

Walter sat down beside her, dropping his body on to the seat with a slack movement. He repeated his former statement.

'They're all bughouse here.'

'You don't like being at Stonygates?'

The young man frowned.

'I simply don't *get* it – that's all! I don't get it. Take this place – the house – the whole set-up. They're rich, these people. They don't need dough – they've got it. And look at the way they live. Cracked antique china and cheap plain stuff all mixed up. No proper upper-class servants – just some casual hired help. Tapestries and drapes and chair-covers all satin and brocade and stuff – and it's falling to pieces! Big silver tea urns and what do you know – all yellow and tarnished for want of cleaning. Mrs Serrocold just doesn't care. Look at that dress she had on last night. Darned under the arms, nearly worn out – and yet she could go to a store and order what she liked. Bond Street or wherever it is. Dough? They're rolling in dough.'

He paused and sat, deliberating.

'I understand being poor. There's nothing much wrong with it. If you're young and strong and ready to work. I never had much money, but I was all set to get where I wanted. I was going to open a garage. I'd got a bit of money put by. I talked to Gina about it. She listened. She seemed to understand. I didn't know much about her. All those girls in uniform, they look about the same. I mean you can't tell from looking at them who's got dough and who hasn't. I thought she was a cut above me, perhaps, education and all that. But it didn't seem to matter. We fell for each other. We got married. I'd got my bit put by and Gina had some too, she told me. We were going to set up a gas station back home – Gina was willing. Just a couple of crazy kids we were – mad about each other. Then that snooty aunt of Gina's started making trouble . . . And Gina wanted to come here to England to see her grandmother. Well, that seemed fair enough. It was her home, and I was curious to see England anyway. I'd heard a lot about it. So we came. Just a visit – that's what I thought.'

The frown became a scowl.

'But it hasn't turned out like that. We're caught up in this crazy business. Why don't we stay here – make our home here – that's what they say? Plenty of jobs for me. Jobs! I don't want a job feeding candy to gangster kids and helping them play at kids' games . . . what's the sense of it all? This place could be swell – *really* swell. Don't people who've got money understand their luck? Don't they understand that most of the world can't have a swell place like this and that they've got one? Isn't it plain crazy to kick your luck when you've got it? I don't mind working if I've got to. But I'll work the way I like and at what I like – and I'll work to get somewhere. This place makes me feel I'm tangled up in a spider's web. And Gina – I can't make Gina out. She's not the same girl I married over in the States. I can't – dang it all – I can't even *talk* to her now. Oh hell!'

Miss Marple said gently:

'I quite see your point of view.'

Wally shot a swift glance at her.

'You're the only one I've shot my mouth off to so far. Most of the time I shut up like a clam. Don't know what it is about you – you're English right enough, really English – but in the durndest way you remind me of my Aunt Betsy back home.'

'Now that's very nice.'

'A lot of sense she had,' Wally continued reflectively. 'Looked as frail as though you could snap her in two, but actually she was tough – yes, sir, I'll say she was tough.'

He got up.

'Sorry talking to you this way,' he apologized. For the first time, Miss Marple saw him smile. It was a very attractive smile, and Wally Hudd was suddenly transfigured from an awkward sulky boy into a handsome and appealing young man. 'Had to get things off my chest, I suppose. But too bad picking on you.'

'Not at all, my dear boy,' said Miss Marple. 'I have a nephew of my own – only, of course, a great deal older than you are.'

Her mind dwelt for a moment on the sophisticated modern writer Raymond West. A greater contrast to Walter Hudd could not have been imagined.

'You've got other company coming,' said Walter Hudd. 'That dame doesn't like me. So I'll quit. So long, ma'am. Thanks for the talk.'

He strode away and Miss Marple watched Mildred Strete coming across the lawn to join her.

II

'I see you've been victimized by that terrible young man,' said Mrs Strete, rather breathlessly, as she sank down on the seat. 'What a tragedy that is.'

'A tragedy?'

'Gina's marriage. It all came about from sending her off to America. I told mother at the time it was most unwise. After all, this is quite a quiet district. We had hardly any raids here. I do so dislike the way many people gave way to panic about their families – and themselves, too, very often.'

'It must have been difficult to decide what was right to do,' said Miss Marple thoughtfully. 'Where children were concerned, I mean. With the prospect of possible invasion, it might have meant their being brought up under a German régime – as well as the danger of bombs.'

'All nonsense,' said Mrs Strete. 'I never had the least doubt that we should win. But mother has always been quite unreasonable where Gina is concerned. The child was always spoilt and indulged in every way. There was absolutely no need to take her away from Italy in the first place.'

'Her father raised no objection, I understand?'

'Oh San Severiano! You know what Italians are. Nothing matters to them but money. He married Pippa for her money, of course.'

'Dear me. I always understood he was very devoted to her and was quite inconsolable at her death.'

'He pretended to be, no doubt. Why mother ever countenanced her marrying a foreigner, I can't imagine. Just the usual American pleasure in a title, I suppose.'

Miss Marple said mildly:

'I always thought that dear Carrie Louise was almost too unworldly in her attitude to life.'

'Oh, I know. I've no patience with it. Mother's fads and whims and idealistic projects. You've no idea, Aunt Jane, of all that it has meant. I can speak with knowledge, of course. I was brought up in the middle of it all.'

It was with a very faint shock that Miss Marple heard herself addressed as Aunt Jane. And yet that had been the convention of those times. Her Christmas presents to Carrie Louise's children were always labelled 'With love from Aunt Jane,' and as 'Aunt Jane' they thought of her, when they thought of her at all. Which was not, Miss Marple supposed, very often.

She looked thoughtfully at the middle-aged woman sitting beside her. At the pursed tight mouth, the deep lines from the nose down, the hands tightly pressed together.

She said gently:

'You must have had – a difficult childhood.'

Mildred Strete turned eager grateful eyes to her.

'Oh I'm so glad that somebody appreciates that. People don't really know what children go through. Pippa, you see, was the pretty one. She was older than I was, too. It was always she who got all the attention. Both father and mother encouraged her to push herself forward – not that she needed any encouragement – to show off. I was always the quiet one. I was shy – Pippa didn't know what shyness was. A child can suffer a great deal, Aunt Jane.'

'I know that,' said Miss Marple.

'"Mildred's so stupid" – that's what Pippa used to say. But I was younger than she was. Naturally I couldn't be expected to keep up with her in lessons. And it's very unfair on a child when her sister is always put in front of her.

'"What a lovely little girl," people used to say to Mamma. They never noticed *me*. And it was Pippa that Papa used to joke and play with. Someone ought to have seen how hard it was on *me*. All the notice and attention going to her. I wasn't old enough to realize that it's *character* that matters.'

Her lips trembled, then hardened again.

'And it was unfair – really unfair – I was their own child. Pippa was only adopted. *I* was the daughter of the house. She was – nobody.'

'Probably they were extra indulgent to her on that account,' said Miss Marple.

'They liked her best,' said Mildred Strete. And added: 'A child whose own parents didn't want her – or more probably illegitimate.'

She went on:

'It's come out in Gina. There's bad blood there. Blood will tell. Lewis can have what theories he likes about environment. Bad blood does tell. Look at Gina.'

'Gina is a very lovely girl,' said Miss Marple.

'Hardly in behaviour,' said Mrs Strete. 'Everyone but mother notices how she is carrying on with Stephen Restarick. Quite disgusting, I call it. Admittedly she made a very unfortunate marriage, but marriage is marriage and one should be prepared to abide by it. After all, she chose to marry that dreadful young man.'

'Is he so dreadful?'

'Oh dear Aunt Jane! He really looks to me quite like a gangster. And so surly and rude. He hardly opens his mouth. And he always looks so raw and uncouth.'

'He is unhappy, I think,' said Miss Marple mildly.

'I really don't know why he should be – apart from Gina's behaviour, I mean. Everything has been done for him here. Lewis has suggested several ways in which he could try to make himself useful – but he prefers to skulk about doing nothing.'

She burst out: 'Oh this whole place is impossible – quite impossible. Lewis thinks of nothing but these horrible young criminals. And mother thinks of nothing but him. Everything Lewis does is right. Look at the state of the garden – the weeds – the overgrowth. And the house – nothing properly done. Oh I know a domestic staff is difficult nowadays, but it can be got. It's not as though there were any shortage of money.

Agatha Christie

It's just that nobody *cares*. If it were *my* house –' She stopped.

'I'm afraid,' said Miss Marple, 'that we have all to face the fact that conditions are different. These large establishments are a great problem. It must be sad for you, in a way, to come back here and find everything so different. Do you really prefer living here to – well – somewhere of your own?'

Mildred Strete flushed.

'After all, it's my home,' she said. 'It was my father's house. Nothing can alter that. I've a right to be here if I choose. And I do choose. If only mother were not so impossible! She won't even buy herself proper clothes. It worries Jolly a lot.'

'I was going to ask you about Miss Bellever.'

'Such a comfort having her here. She adores mother. She's been with her a long time now – she came in John Restarick's time. And was wonderful, I believe, during the whole sad business. I expect you heard that he ran away with a dreadful Yugoslavian woman – a most abandoned creature. She'd had any amount of lovers, I believe. Mother was very fine and dignified about it all. Divorced him as quietly as possible. Even went so far as to have the Restarick boys for their holidays – quite unnecessary, really, other arrangements could have been made. It would have been unthinkable, of course, to have let them go to their father and that

72

woman. Anyway, mother had them here . . . And Miss Bellever stood by all through things and was a tower of strength. I sometimes think she makes mother even more vague than she need be, by doing all the practical things herself. But I really don't know what mother would do without her.'

She paused and then remarked in a tone of surprise:

'Here is Lewis. How odd. He seldom comes out in the garden.'

Mr Serrocold came towards them in the same single-minded way that he did everything. He appeared not to notice Mildred, because it was only Miss Marple who was in his mind.

'I'm so sorry,' he said. 'I wanted to take you round our institution and show you everything. Caroline asked me to. Unfortunately I have to go off to Liverpool. The case of that boy and the railway parcels office. But Maverick will take you. He'll be here in a few minutes. I shan't be back until the day after tomorrow. It will be splendid if we can get them not to prosecute.'

Mildred Strete got up and walked away. Lewis Serrocold did not notice her go. His earnest eyes gazed at Miss Marple through thick glasses.

'You see,' he said, 'the Magistrates nearly always take the wrong view. Sometimes they're too severe, but sometimes they're too lenient. If these boys get a sentence of a few months it's no deterrent – they get a kind of a kick out of it, even. Boast about it to their girl friends. But a severe sentence often sobers them. They realize that the game isn't worth it. Or else it's better not to serve a prison sentence at all. Corrective training – constructional training like we have here –'

Miss Marple interrupted him.

'Mr Serrocold,' she said. 'Are you quite satisfied about young Mr Lawson. Is he – is he quite normal?'

A disturbed expression appeared on Lewis Serrocold's face.

'I do hope he's not relapsing. What has he been saying?'

'He told me that he was Winston Churchill's son –'

'Of course – of course. The usual statements. He's illegitimate, as you've probably guessed, poor lad, and of very humble beginnings. He was a case recommended to me by a Society in London. He'd assaulted a man in the street who he said was spying on him. All very typical – Dr Maverick will tell you. I went into his case history. Mother was of a poor class but a respectable family in Plymouth. Father a sailor – she didn't even know his name . . . Child brought up in difficult circumstances. Started romancing about his father and later about himself. Wore uniform and decorations he wasn't entitled to – all quite typical. But Maverick considers the prognosis hopeful. If we can give him confidence in himself. I've given him responsibility here, tried to make him appreciate that it's not a man's birth that matters but what he *is*. I've tried to give him confidence in his own ability. The improvement was marked. I was very happy about him. And now you say –'

He shook his head.

'Mightn't he be dangerous, Mr Serrocold?'

'Dangerous? I don't think he has shown any suicidal tendencies.'

'I wasn't thinking of suicide. He talked to me of enemies – of persecution. Isn't that, forgive me – a dangerous sign?'

'I don't really think it has reached such a pitch. But I'll speak to Maverick. So far, he has been hopeful – very hopeful.'

He looked at his watch.

'I must go. Ah, here is our dear Jolly. She will take charge of you.'

Miss Bellever, arriving briskly, said, 'The car is at the door, Mr Serrocold. Dr Maverick rang through from the Institute. I said I would bring Miss Marple over. He will meet us at the gates.'

'Thank you. I must go. My briefcase?'

'In the car, Mr Serrocold.'

Lewis Serrocold hurried away. Looking after him, Miss Bellever said:

'Some day that man will drop dead in his tracks. It's against human nature never to relax or rest. He only sleeps four hours a night.'

'He is very devoted to this cause,' said Miss Marple.

'Never thinks of anything else,' said Miss Bellever grimly. 'Never dreams of looking after his wife or considering her in any way. She's a sweet creature, as you know, Miss Marple, and she ought to have love and attention. But nothing's thought of or considered here except a lot of whining boys and young men who want to live easily and dishonestly and don't care about the idea of doing a little hard work. What about the decent boys from decent homes? Why isn't something done for them? Honesty just isn't interesting to cranks like Mr Serrocold and Dr Maverick and all the bunch of half-baked sentimentalists we've got here. I and my brothers were brought up the hard way, Miss Marple, and we weren't encouraged to whine. Soft, that's what the world is nowadays!'

They had crossed the garden and passed through a palisaded gate and had come to the arched gate which Eric Gulbrandsen had erected as an entrance to his College, a sturdily built, hideous, red brick building.

Dr Maverick, looking, Miss Marple decided, distinctly abnormal himself, came out to meet them.

'Thank you, Miss Bellever,' he said. 'Now, Miss – er – oh yes, Miss Marple – I'm sure you're going to be interested in what we're doing here. In our splendid approach to this great problem. Mr Serrocold is a man of great insight – great vision. And we've got Sir John Stillwell behind us – my old chief. He was at the Home Office until he retired and his influence turned the scales in getting this started. It's a *medical* problem – that's what we've got to get the legal authorities to understand. Psychiatry came into its own in the war. The one positive good that did come out of it – Now first of all I want you to see our initial approach to the problem. Look up –'

Miss Marple looked up at the words carved over the large arched doorway:

RECOVER HOPE ALL YE WHO ENTER HERE

'Isn't that splendid! Isn't that just the right note to strike. You don't want to scold these lads – or punish them. That's what they're hankering after half the time, punishment. We want to make them feel what fine fellows they are.'

'Like Edgar Lawson?' said Miss Marple.

'Interesting case, that. Have you been talking to him?'

'He has been talking to me,' said Miss Marple. She added apologetically, 'I wondered if, perhaps, he isn't a little *mad*?'

Agatha Christie

Dr Maverick laughed cheerfully.

'We're all mad, dear lady,' he said as he ushered her in through the door. 'That's the secret of existence. We're all a little mad.'

Chapter 6

I

On the whole it was rather an exhausting day.

Enthusiasm in itself can be extremely wearing, Miss Marple thought. She felt vaguely dissatisfied with herself and her own reactions. There was a pattern here – perhaps several patterns, and yet she herself could obtain no clear glimpse of it or them. Any vague disquietude she felt centred round the pathetic but inconspicuous personality of Edgar Lawson. If she could only find in her memory the right parallel.

Painstakingly she rejected the curious behaviour of Mr Selkirk's delivery van – the absent-minded postman – the gardener who worked on Whit Monday – and that very curious affair of the summer weight combinations.

Something that she could not quite put her finger on was wrong about Edgar Lawson – something that went beyond the observed and admitted facts. But for the life of her, Miss Marple did not see how that wrongness, whatever it was, affected her friend Carrie Louise. In the confused patterns of life at Stonygates people's troubles and desires impinged on each other. But none of them (again as far as she could see) impinged on Carrie Louise.

Carrie Louise . . . Suddenly Miss Marple realized that it was she alone, except for the absent Ruth, who used that name. To her husband, she was Caroline. To Miss Bellever, Cara. Stephen Restarick usually addressed her as Madonna. To Wally she was formally Mrs Serrocold, and Gina elected to address her as Grandam – a mixture, she had explained, of Grande Dame and Grandmamma.

Was there some significance, perhaps, in the various names that were found for Caroline Louise Serrocold? Was she to all of them a symbol and not quite a real person?

When on the following morning Carrie Louise, dragging her feet a little as she walked, came and sat down on the garden seat beside her friend and asked her what she was thinking about, Miss Marple replied promptly:

'You, Carrie Louise.'

'What about me?'

'Tell me honestly – is there anything here that worries you?'

'Worries me?' The woman raised wondering clear blue eyes. 'But Jane, what should worry me?'

'Well, most of us have worries.' Miss Marple's eyes twinkled a little. 'I have. Slugs, you know – and the difficulty of getting linen properly darned – and not being able to get sugar candy for making my damson gin. Oh, lots of little things – it seems unnatural that you shouldn't have any worries at all.'

'I suppose I must have really,' said Mrs Serrocold vaguely. 'Lewis works too hard, and Stephen forgets his meals slaving at the theatre, and Gina is very jumpy – but I've never been able to alter people – I don't see how you can. So it wouldn't be any good worrying, would it?'

'Mildred's not very happy, either, is she?'

'Oh no,' said Carrie Louise. 'Mildred never is happy. She wasn't as a child. Quite unlike Pippa, who was always radiant.'

'Perhaps,' suggested Miss Marple, 'Mildred had cause not to be happy?'

Carrie Louise said quietly:

'Because of being jealous? Yes, I daresay. But people don't really need a cause for feeling what they do feel. They're just made that way. Don't you think so, Jane?'

Miss Marple thought briefly of Miss Moncrieff, a slave to a tyrannical invalid mother. Poor Miss

81

Moncrieff who longed for travel and to see the world. And of how St Mary Mead in a decorous way had rejoiced when Mrs Moncrieff was laid in the church-yard and Miss Moncrieff, with a nice little income, was free at last. And of how Miss Moncrieff, starting on her travels, had got no farther than Hyères where, calling to see one of 'mother's oldest friends', she had been so moved by the plight of an elderly hypochondriac that she had cancelled her travel reservations and taken up her abode in the villa to be bullied, over-worked, and to long wistfully, once more, for the joys of a wider horizon.

Miss Marple said:

'I expect you're right, Carrie Louise.'

'Of course my being so free from cares is partly due to Jolly. Dear Jolly. She came to me when Johnnie and I were just married and was wonderful from the first. She takes care of me as though I were a baby and quite helpless. She'd do anything for me. I feel quite ashamed sometimes. I really believe Jolly would murder someone for me, Jane. Isn't that an awful thing to say?'

'She's certainly very devoted,' agreed Miss Marple.

'She gets so indignant.' Mrs Serrocold's silvery laugh rang out. 'She'd like me to be always ordering won-derful clothes, and surrounding myself with luxuries, and she thinks everybody ought to put me first and to dance attendance on me. She's the one person who's absolutely unimpressed by Lewis's enthusiasm. All our poor boys are in her view pampered young criminals and not worth taking trouble over. She thinks this place is damp and bad for my rheumatism, and that I ought to go to Egypt or somewhere warm and dry.'

'Do you suffer much from rheumatism?'

'It's got much worse lately. I find it difficult to walk. Horrid cramps in my legs. Oh well –' again there came that bewitching elfin smile, 'age must tell.'

Miss Bellever came out of the French windows and hurried across to them.

'A telegram, Cara, just come over the telephone. *Arriving this afternoon, Christian Gulbrandsen.*'

'Christian?' Carrie Louise looked very surprised. 'I'd no idea he was in England.'

'The oak suite, I suppose?'

'Yes, please, Jolly. Then there will be no stairs.'

Miss Bellever nodded and turned back to the house.

'Christian Gulbrandsen is my stepson,' said Carrie Louise. 'Eric's eldest son. Actually he's two years older than I am. He's one of the trustees of the Institute – the principal trustee. How very annoying that Lewis is away. Christian hardly ever stays longer than one night. He's an immensely busy man. And there are sure to be so many things they would want to discuss.'

Christian Gulbrandsen arrived that afternoon in time

for tea. He was a big heavy-featured man, with a slow methodical way of talking. He greeted Carrie Louise with every sign of affection.

'And how is our little Carrie Louise? You do not look a day older. Not a day.'

His hands on her shoulders – he stood smiling down at her. A hand tugged his sleeve.

'Christian!'

'Ah,' he turned – 'it is Mildred? How are you, Mildred?'

'I've not really been at all well lately.'

'That is bad. That is bad.'

There was a strong resemblance between Christian Gulbrandsen and his half-sister Mildred. There was nearly thirty years' difference in age and they might easily have been taken for father and daughter. Mildred herself seemed particularly pleased by his arrival. She was flushed and talkative, and had talked repeatedly during the day of 'my brother,' 'my brother Christian,' 'my brother Mr Gulbrandsen.'

'And how is little Gina?' said Gulbrandsen, turning to that young woman. 'You and your husband are still here, then?'

'Yes. We've quite settled down, haven't we, Wally?'

'Looks like it,' said Wally.

Gulbrandsen's small shrewd eyes seemed to sum

up Wally quickly. Wally, as usual, looked sullen and unfriendly.

'So here I am with all the family again,' said Gulbrandsen.

His voice displayed a rather determined geniality – but in actual fact, Miss Marple thought, he was not feeling particularly genial. There was a grim set to his lips and a certain preoccupation in his manner.

Introduced to Miss Marple, he swept a keen look over her as though measuring and appraising this newcomer.

'We'd no idea you were in England, Christian,' said Mrs Serrocold.

'No, I came over rather unexpectedly.'

'It is too bad that Lewis is away. How long can you stay?'

'I meant to go tomorrow. When will Lewis be back?'

'Tomorrow afternoon or evening.'

'It seems then that I must stay another night.'

'If you'd only let us know –'

'My dear Carrie Louise, my arrangements, they were made very suddenly.'

'You will stay to see Lewis?'

'Yes, it is necessary that I see Lewis.'

Miss Bellever said to Miss Marple: 'Mr Gulbrandsen and Mr Serrocold are both trustees of the Gulbrandsen

Institute. The others are the Bishop of Cromer and Mr Gilfoy.'

Presumably, then, it was on business concerned with the Gulbrandsen Institute that Christian Gulbrandsen had come to Stonygates. It seemed to be assumed so by Miss Bellever and everyone else. And yet Miss Marple wondered.

Once or twice the old man cast a thoughtful puzzled look at Carrie Louise when she was not aware of it – a look that puzzled Carrie Louise's watching friend. From Carrie Louise he shifted his gaze to the others, examining them one and all with a kind of covert appraisal that seemed distinctly odd.

After tea, Miss Marple withdrew tactfully from the others to the library, but rather to her surprise when she had settled herself with her knitting, Christian Gulbrandsen came in and sat down beside her.

'You are a very old friend, I think, of our dear Carrie Louise?' he said.

'We were at school together in Italy, Mr Gulbrandsen. Many many years ago.'

'Ah yes. And you are fond of her?'

'Yes, indeed,' said Miss Marple warmly.

'So, I think, is everyone. Yes, I truly think that. It should be so. For she is a very dear and enchanting person. Always, since my father married her, I and my brothers have loved her very much. She has been to us like a very dear sister. She was a faithful wife to my father and loyal to all his ideas. She has never thought of herself, but put the welfare of others first.'

'She has always been an idealist,' said Miss Marple.

'An idealist? Yes. Yes, that is so. And therefore it may be that she does not truly appreciate the evil that there is in the world.'

Miss Marple looked at him, surprised. His face was very stern.

'Tell me,' he said. 'How is her health?'

Again Miss Marple felt surprised.

'She seems to me very well – apart from arthritis – or rheumatism.'

'Rheumatism? Yes. And her heart? Her heart is good?'

'As far as I know.' Miss Marple was still more surprised. 'But until yesterday I had not seen her for many years. If you want to know the state of her health, you should ask somebody in the house here. Miss Bellever, for instance.'

'Miss Bellever – Yes, Miss Bellever. Or Mildred?'

'Or, as you say, Mildred.'

Miss Marple was faintly embarrassed.

Christian Gulbrandsen was staring at her very hard.

'There is not between the mother and daughter a very great sympathy, would you say?'

'No, I don't think there is.'

'I agree. It is a pity – her only child, but there it is. Now this Miss Bellever, you think, is really attached to her?'

'Very much so.'

'And Carrie Louise leans on this Miss Bellever?'

'I think so.'

Christian Gulbrandsen was frowning. He spoke as though more to himself than to Miss Marple.

'There is the little Gina – but she is so young. It is difficult –' He broke off. 'Sometimes,' he said simply, 'it is hard to know what is best to be done. I wish very much to act for the best. I am particularly anxious that no harm and no unhappiness should come to that dear lady. But it is not easy – not easy at all.'

Mrs Strete came into the room at that moment.

'Oh, there you are, Christian. We were wondering where you were. Dr Maverick wants to know if you would like to go over anything with him.'

'That is the new young doctor here? No – no, I will wait until Lewis returns.'

'He's waiting in Lewis's study. Shall I tell him –'

'I will have a word with him myself.'

Gulbrandsen hurried out. Mildred Strete stared after him and then stared at Miss Marple.

'I wonder if anything is wrong. Christian is very unlike himself . . . Did he say anything –'

'He only asked me about your mother's health.'

'Her health? Why should he ask you about that?'

Mildred spoke sharply, her large square face flushing unbecomingly.

'I really don't know.'

'Mother's health is perfectly good. Surprisingly so for a woman of her age. Much better than mine as far as that goes.' She paused a moment before saying: 'I hope you told him so?'

'I don't really know anything about it,' said Miss Marple. 'He asked me about her heart.'

'Her *heart*?'

'Yes.'

'There's nothing wrong with mother's heart. Nothing at all!'

'I'm delighted to hear you say so, my dear.'

'What on earth put all these queer ideas into Christian's head?'

'I've no idea,' said Miss Marple.

Chapter 7

I

The next day passed uneventfully to all appearances, yet to Miss Marple it seemed that there were signs of an inner tension. Christian Gulbrandsen spent his morning with Dr Maverick in going round the Institute and in discussing the general results of the Institute's policy. In the early afternoon Gina took him for a drive, and after that Miss Marple noticed that he induced Miss Bellever to show him something in the gardens. It seemed to her that it was a pretext for ensuring a *tête-à-tête* with that grim woman. And yet, if Christian Gulbrandsen's unexpected visit had only to do with business matters, why this wish for Miss Bellever's company, since the latter dealt only with the domestic side of Stonygates?

But in all this, Miss Marple could tell herself that she was being fanciful. The one really disturbing incident of the day happened about four o'clock. She had rolled up her knitting and had gone out in the garden to take a little stroll before tea. Rounding a straggling rhododendron she came upon Edgar Lawson, who was striding along muttering to himself and who nearly ran into her.

He said, 'I beg your pardon,' hastily, but Miss Marple was startled by the queer staring expression of his eyes.

'Aren't you feeling well, Mr Lawson?'

'Well? How should I be feeling well? I've had a shock – a terrible shock.'

'What kind of a shock?'

The young man gave a swift glance past her, and then a sharp uneasy glance to either side. His doing so gave Miss Marple a nervous feeling.

'Shall I tell you?' He looked at her doubtfully. 'I don't know. I don't really *know*. I've been so spied upon.'

Miss Marple made up her mind. She took him firmly by the arm.

'If we walk down this path . . . There, now, there are no trees or bushes near. Nobody can overhear.'

'No – no, you're right.' He drew a deep breath, bent his head and almost whispered his next words. 'I've made a discovery. A terrible discovery.'

Edgar Lawson began to shake all over. He was almost weeping.

'To have trusted someone! To have believed . . .

and it was lies – all lies. Lies to keep me from finding out the truth. I can't bear it. It's too wicked. You see, he was the one person I trusted, and now to find out that all the time he's been at the bottom of it all. It's *he* who's been my enemy! It's *he* who has been having me followed about and spied upon. But he can't get away with it any more. I shall speak out. I shall tell him I know what he has been doing.'

'Who is "*he*"?' demanded Miss Marple.

Edgar Lawson drew himself up to his full height. He might have looked pathetic and dignified. But actually he only looked ridiculous.

'I'm speaking of my father.'

'Viscount Montgomery – or do you mean Winston Churchill?'

Edgar threw her a glance of scorn.

'They let me think that – just to keep me from guessing the truth. But I know now. I've got a friend – a real friend. A friend who tells me the truth and lets me know just how I've been deceived. Well, my father will have to reckon with *me*. I'll throw his lies in his face! I'll challenge him with the truth. We'll see what he's got to say to that.'

And suddenly breaking away, Edgar went off at a run and disappeared in the park.

Her face grave, Miss Marple went back to the house.

'We're all a little mad, dear lady,' Dr Maverick had said.

But it seemed to her that in Edgar's case it went rather further than that.

II

Lewis Serrocold arrived back at six-thirty. He stopped the car at the gates and walked to the house through the park. Looking out of her window, Miss Marple saw Christian Gulbrandsen go out to meet him and the two men, having greeted one another, turned and paced to and fro up and down the terrace.

Miss Marple had been careful to bring her bird glasses with her. At this moment she brought them into action. Was there, or was there not, a flight of siskins by that far clump of trees?

She noted as the glasses swept down before rising that both men were looking seriously disturbed. Miss Marple leant out a little farther. Scraps of conversation floated up to her now and then. If either of the men should look up, it would be quite clear that an enraptured bird watcher had her attention fixed on a point far removed from their conversation.

'. . . how to spare Carrie Louise the knowledge –' Gulbrandsen was saying.

The next time they passed below, Lewis Serrocold was speaking.

'. . . if it *can* be kept from her. I agree that it is she who must be considered . . .'

Other faint snatches came to the listener.

'– Really serious –' '– not justified –' '– too big a responsibility to take –' '– we should, perhaps, take outside advice –'

Finally Miss Marple heard Christian Gulbrandsen say:

'Ach, it grows cold. We must go inside.'

Miss Marple drew her head in through the window with a puzzled expression. What she had heard was too fragmentary to be easily pieced together – but it served to confirm that vague apprehension that had been gradually growing upon her and about which Ruth Van Rydock had been so positive.

Whatever was wrong at Stonygates, it definitely affected Carrie Louise.

III

Dinner that evening was a somewhat constrained meal. Both Gulbrandsen and Lewis were absent-minded and absorbed in their own thoughts. Walter Hudd glowered even more than usual, and for once Gina and Stephen seemed to have little to say either to each other or to the company at large. Conversation was mostly sustained by Dr Maverick, who had a lengthy technical discussion with Mr Baumgarten, one of the Occupational Therapists.

When they moved into the hall after dinner, Christian Gulbrandsen excused himself almost at once. He said he had an important letter to write.

'So if you will forgive me, dear Carrie Louise, I will go now to my room.'

'You have all you want there? Jolly?'

'Yes, yes. Everything. A typewriter, I asked, and one has been put there. Miss Bellever has been most kind and attentive.'

He left the Great Hall by the door on the left which led past the foot of the main staircase and along a corridor, at the end of which was a suite of bedroom and bathroom.

When he had gone out Carrie Louise said:

'Not going down to the theatre tonight, Gina?'

The girl shook her head. She went over and sat by the window overlooking the front drive and the court.

Stephen glanced at her, then strolled over to the big grand piano. He sat down at it and strummed very softly – a queer melancholy little tune. The two Occupational Therapists, Mr Baumgarten and Mr Lacy, and Dr Maverick, said goodnight and left. Walter turned on the switch of a reading lamp and with a crackling noise half the lights in the hall went out.

He growled.

'That darned switch is always faulty. I'll go and put a new fuse in.'

He left the Hall and Carrie Louise murmured, 'Wally's so clever with electrical gadgets and things like that. You remember how he fixed that toaster?'

'It seems to be all he does do here,' said Mildred Strete. 'Mother, have you taken your tonic?'

Miss Bellever looked annoyed.

'I declare I completely forgot tonight.' She jumped up and went into the dining-room, returning presently with a small glass containing a little rose-coloured fluid.

Smiling a little, Carrie Louise held out an obedient hand.

'Such horrid stuff and nobody lets me forget it,' she said, making a wry face.

And then, rather unexpectedly, Lewis Serrocold said: 'I don't think I should take it tonight, my dear. I'm not sure it really agrees with you.'

Quietly, but with that controlled energy always so apparent in him, he took the glass from Miss Bellever and put it down on the big oak Welsh dresser.

Miss Bellever said sharply:

'Really, Mr Serrocold, I can't agree with you there. Mrs Serrocold has been very much better since –'

She broke off and turned sharply.

The front door was pushed violently open and allowed to swing to with a crash. Edgar Lawson came into the big dim Hall with the air of a star performer making a triumphal entry.

He stood in the middle of the floor and struck an attitude.

It was almost ridiculous – but not quite ridiculous.

Edgar said theatrically:

'So I have found you, O mine enemy!'

He said it to Lewis Serrocold.

Mr Serrocold looked mildly astonished.

'Why, Edgar, what is the matter?'

'You can say that to me – you!' You know what's the matter. You've been deceiving me, spying on me, working with my enemies against me.'

Lewis took him by the arm.

'Now, now, my dear lad, don't excite yourself. Tell me all about it quietly. Come into my office.'

He led him across the Hall and through a door on the right, closing it behind him. After he had done so, there was another sound, the sharp sound of a key being turned in the lock.

Miss Bellever looked at Miss Marple, the same idea in both their minds. *It was not Lewis Serrocold who had turned the key.*

Miss Bellever said sharply: 'That young man is

just about to go off his head in my opinion. It isn't safe.'

Mildred said: 'He's a most unbalanced young man – and absolutely ungrateful for everything that's been done for him – you ought to put your foot down, Mother.'

With a faint sigh Carrie Louise murmured:

'There's no harm in him really. He's fond of Lewis. He's very fond of him.'

Miss Marple looked at her curiously. There had been no fondness in the expression that Edgar had turned on Lewis Serrocold a few moments previously, very far from it. She wondered, as she wondered before, if Carrie Louise deliberately turned her back on reality.

Gina said sharply:

'He had something in his pocket. Edgar, I mean. Playing with it.'

Stephen murmured as he took his hands from the keys:

'In a film it would certainly have been a revolver.'

Miss Marple coughed.

'I think you know,' she said apologetically, 'it *was* a revolver.'

From behind the closed door of Lewis's office the sound of voices had been plainly discernible. Now, suddenly, they became clearly audible. Edgar Lawson shouted whilst Lewis Serrocold's voice kept its even reasonable note.

'Lies – lies – lies, all lies. *You*'re my father. I'm *your* son. You've deprived me of my rights. *I* ought to own this place. You hate me – you want to get rid of me!'

There was a soothing murmur from Lewis and then the hysterical voice rose still higher. It screamed out foul epithets. Edgar seemed rapidly losing control of himself. Occasional words came from Lewis – 'calm – just be calm – you know none of this is true –' But they seemed not to soothe, but on the contrary to enrage the young man still further.

Insensibly everyone in the hall was silent, listening intently to what went on behind the locked door of Lewis's study.

'I'll make you listen to me,' yelled Edgar. 'I'll take that supercilious expression off your face. I'll have revenge, I tell you. Revenge for all you've made me suffer.'

The other voice came curtly, unlike Lewis's usual unemotional tones.

'Put that revolver down!'

Gina cried sharply:

'Edgar will kill him. He's crazy. Can't we get the police or something?'

Carrie Louise, still unmoved, said softly:

'There's no need to worry, Gina. Edgar loves Lewis. He's just dramatizing himself, that's all.'

Edgar's voice sounded through the door in a laugh that Miss Marple had to admit sounded definitely insane.

'Yes, I've got a revolver – and it's loaded. No, don't speak, don't move. You're going to hear me out. It's you who started this conspiracy against me and now you're going to pay for it.'

What sounded like the report of a firearm made them all start, but Carrie Louise said:

'It's all right, it's outside – in the park somewhere.'

Behind the locked door, Edgar was raving in a high screaming voice.

'You sit there looking at me – looking at me – pretending to be unmoved. Why don't you get down on your knees and beg for mercy? I'm going to shoot, I tell you. I'm going to shoot you dead! I'm your son – your unacknowledged despised son – you wanted me hidden away, out of the world altogether, perhaps. You set your spies to follow me – to hound me down – you plotted against me. You, my father! My father. I'm only a bastard, aren't I? Only a bastard. You went on filling me up with lies. Pretending to be kind to me, and all the time – all the time – You're not fit to live. I won't let you live.'

Again there came a stream of obscene profanity.

Somewhere during the scene Miss Marple was conscious of Miss Bellever saying:

'We must *do* something,' and leaving the Hall.

Edgar seemed to pause for breath and then he shouted out:

'You're going to die – to *die*. You're going to die *now*. Take *that*, you devil, and *that*!'

Two sharp cracks rang out – not in the park this time, but definitely behind the locked door.

Somebody, Miss Marple thought it was Mildred, cried out:

'Oh God, what shall we do?'

There was a thud from inside the room and then a sound, almost more terrible than what had gone before, the sound of slow heavy sobbing.

Somebody strode past Miss Marple and started shaking and rattling the door.

It was Stephen Restarick.

'Open the door. Open the door,' he shouted.

Miss Bellever came back into the Hall. In her hand she held an assortment of keys.

'Try some of these,' she said breathlessly.

At that moment the fused lights came on again. The Hall sprang into life again after its eerie dimness.

Stephen Restarick began trying the keys.

They heard the inside key fall out as he did so.

Inside that wild desperate sobbing went on.

Walter Hudd, coming lazily back into the Hall, stopped dead and demanded:

'Say, what's going on round here?'

Mildred said tearfully:

'That awful crazy young man has shot Mr Serrocold.'

'Please.' It was Carrie Louise who spoke. She got up and came across to the study door. Very gently she pushed Stephen Restarick aside. 'Let me speak to him.'

She called – very softly – 'Edgar . . . Edgar . . . let me in, will you? Please, Edgar.'

They heard the key fitted into the lock. It turned and the door was slowly opened.

But it was not Edgar who opened it. It was Lewis Serrocold. He was breathing hard as though he had been running, but otherwise he was unmoved.

'It's all right, dearest,' he said. 'Dearest, it's quite all right.'

'We thought you'd been shot,' said Miss Bellever gruffly.

Lewis Serrocold frowned. He said with a trifle of asperity:

'Of course I haven't been shot.'

They could see into the study by now. Edgar Lawson had collapsed by the desk. He was sobbing and gasping. The revolver lay on the floor where it had dropped from his hand.

'But we heard the shots,' said Mildred.

'Oh yes, he fired twice.'

'And he missed you?'

'Of course he missed me,' snapped Lewis.

Miss Marple did not consider that there was any of course about it. The shots must have been fired at fairly close range.

Lewis Serrocold said irritably:

'Where's Maverick? It's Maverick we need.'

Miss Bellever said:

'I'll get him. Shall I ring up the police as well?'

'Police? Certainly not.'

'Of course we must ring up the police,' said Mildred. 'He's dangerous.'

'Nonsense,' said Lewis Serrocold. 'Poor lad. Does he look dangerous?'

At the moment he did not look dangerous. He looked young and pathetic and rather repulsive.

His voice had lost its carefully acquired accent.

'I didn't mean to do it,' he groaned. 'I dunno what came over me – talking all that stuff – I must have been mad.'

Mildred sniffed.

'I really must have been mad. I didn't mean to. Please, Mr Serrocold, I really didn't mean to.'

Lewis Serrocold patted him on the shoulder.

'That's all right, my boy. No damage done.'

'I might have killed you, Mr Serrocold.'

Walter Hudd walked across the room and peered at the wall behind the desk.

'The bullets went in here,' he said. His eye dropped to the desk and the chair behind it. 'Must have been a near miss,' he said grimly.

'I lost my head. I didn't rightly know what I was doing. I thought he'd done me out of my rights. I thought –'

Miss Marple put in the question she had been wanting to ask for some time.

'Who told you,' she asked, 'that Mr Serrocold was your father?'

Just for a second a sly expression peeped out of Edgar's distracted face. It was there and gone in a flash.

'Nobody,' he said. 'I just got it into my head.'

Walter Hudd was staring down at the revolver where it lay on the floor.

'Where the hell did you get that gun?' he demanded.

'Gun?' Edgar stared down at it.

'Looks mighty like my gun,' said Walter. He stooped down and picked it up. 'By heck, it *is*! You took it out of my room, you creeping louse, you.'

Lewis Serrocold interposed between the cringing Edgar and the menacing American.

'All this can be gone into later,' he said. 'Ah, here's Maverick. Take a look at him, will you, Maverick?'

105

Dr Maverick advanced upon Edgar with a kind of professional zest.

'This won't do, Edgar,' he said. 'This won't do, you know.'

'He's a dangerous lunatic,' said Mildred sharply. 'He's been shooting off a revolver and raving. He only just missed my stepfather.'

Edgar gave a little yelp and Dr Maverick said reprovingly:

'Careful, please, Mrs Strete.'

'I'm sick of all this. Sick of the way you all go on here! I tell you this man's a lunatic.'

With a bound Edgar wrenched himself away from Dr Maverick and fell to the floor at Serrocold's feet.

'Help me. Help me. Don't let them take me away and shut me up. Don't let them . . .'

An unpleasing scene, Miss Marple thought.

Mildred said angrily, 'I tell you he's –'

Her mother said soothingly:

'Please Mildred. Not now. He's suffering.'

Walter muttered:

'Suffering cripes. They're all cuckoo round here.'

'I'll take charge of him,' said Dr Maverick. 'You come with me, Edgar. Bed and a sedative – and we'll talk everything out in the morning. Now you trust me, don't you?'

Rising to his feet and trembling a little, Edgar looked

doubtfully at the young doctor and then at Mildred Strete.

'She said – I was a lunatic.'

'No, no, you're not a lunatic.'

Miss Bellever's footsteps rang purposefully across the Hall. She came in with her lips pursed together and a flushed face.

'I've telephoned the police,' she said grimly. 'They will be here in a few minutes.'

Carrie Louise cried, 'Jolly!' in tones of dismay.

Edgar uttered a wail.

Lewis Serrocold frowned angrily.

'I told you, Jolly, I did *not* want the police summoned. This is a medical matter.'

'That's as may be,' said Miss Bellever. 'I've my own opinion. But I had to call the police. Mr Gulbrandsen's been shot dead.'

Chapter 8

I

It was a moment or two before anyone took in what she was saying.

Carrie Louise said incredulously:

'Christian shot? Dead? Oh, surely, that's impossible.'

'If you don't believe me,' said Miss Bellever, pursing her lips, and addressing not so much Carrie Louise, as the assembled company, 'go and look for yourselves.'

She was angry. And her anger sounded in the crisp sharpness of her voice.

Slowly, unbelievingly, Carrie Louise took a step towards the door. Lewis Serrocold put a hand on her shoulder.

'No, dearest, let me go.'

He went out through the doorway. Dr Maverick, with a doubtful glance at Edgar, followed him. Miss Bellever went with them.

Miss Marple gently urged Carrie Louise into a chair. She sat down, her eyes looking hurt and stricken.

'Christian – shot?' she said again.

It was the bewildered hurt tone of a child.

Walter Hudd remained close to Edgar Lawson, glowering down at him. In his hand he held the gun that he had picked up from the floor.

Mrs Serrocold said in a wondering voice:

'But who could possibly want to shoot *Christian*?'

It was not a question that demanded an answer.

Walter muttered under his breath:

'Nuts! The whole lot of them.'

Stephen had moved protectively closer to Gina. Her young startled face was the most vivid thing in the room.

Suddenly the front door opened and a rush of cold air together with a man in a big overcoat came in.

The heartiness of his greeting seemed incredibly shocking.

'Hallo, everybody, what's going on tonight? A lot of fog on the road. I had to go dead slow.'

For a startled moment, Miss Marple thought that she was seeing double. Surely the same man could not be standing by Gina and coming in by the door. Then she realized that it was only a likeness and not, when you looked closely, such a very strong likeness. The two men were clearly brothers with a strong family resemblance, but no more.

Where Stephen Restarick was thin to the point of emaciation the newcomer was sleek. The big coat with the astrakhan collar fitted the sleekness of body snugly. A handsome young man, and one who bore upon him the authority and good humour of success.

But Miss Marple noted one thing about him. His eyes, as he entered the hall, looked immediately at Gina.

He said, a little doubtfully:

'You *did* expect me? You got my wire?'

He was speaking now to Carrie Louise. He came towards her.

Almost mechanically, she put her hand out to him. He took it and kissed it gently. It was an affectionate act of homage, not a mere theatrical courtesy.

She murmured:

'Of course, Alex dear – of course. Only, you see – things have been happening –'

'Happening?'

Mildred gave the information, gave it with a kind of grim relish that Miss Marple found distasteful.

'Christian Gulbrandsen,' she said. 'My brother Christian Gulbrandsen has been found shot dead.'

'Good God,' Alex registered a more than life-size dismay. 'Suicide, do you mean?'

Carrie Louise moved swiftly.

'Oh no,' she said. 'It couldn't be suicide. Not *Christian*! Oh no.'

'Uncle Christian would never shoot himself, I'm sure,' said Gina.

Alex Restarick looked from one person to the other. From his brother Stephen he received a short confirmative nod. Walter Hudd stared back at him with faint resentment. Alex's eyes rested on Miss Marple with a sudden frown. It was as though he had found some unwanted prop on a stage set.

He looked as though he would like her explained. But nobody explained her, and Miss Marple continued to look an old, fluffy and sweetly bewildered old lady.

'When?' asked Alex. 'When did this happen, I mean?'

'Just before you arrived,' said Gina. 'About – oh three or four minutes ago, I suppose. Why, of course, we actually heard the shot. Only we didn't notice it – not really.'

'Didn't notice it? Why not?'

'Well, you see, there were other things going on . . .' Gina spoke rather hesitantly.

'Sure were,' said Walter with emphasis.

Juliet Bellever came into the Hall by the door from the library.

'Mr Serrocold suggests that we should all wait in the

library. It would be convenient for the police. Except for Mrs Serrocold. You've had a shock, Cara. I've ordered some hot bottles to be put in your bed. I'll take you up and –'

Rising to her feet, Carrie Louise shook her head.

'I must see Christian first,' she said.

'Oh no, dear. Don't upset yourself –'

Carrie Louise put her very gently to one side.

'Dear Jolly – you don't understand.' She looked round and said, 'Jane?'

Miss Marple had already moved towards her.

'Come with me, will you, Jane.'

They moved together towards the door. Dr Maverick, coming in, almost collided with them.

Miss Bellever exclaimed:

'Dr Maverick. Do stop her. So foolish.'

Carrie Louise looked calmly at the young doctor. She even gave a tiny smile.

Dr Maverick said: 'You want to go and – see him?'

'I must.'

'I see.' He stood aside. 'If you feel you must, Mrs Serrocold. But afterwards, please go and lie down and let Miss Bellever look after you. At the moment you do not feel the shock, but I assure you that you will do so.'

'Yes. I expect you are right. I will be quite sensible. Come, Jane.'

Agatha Christie

The two women moved out through the door, past the foot of the main staircase and along the corridor, past the dining-room on the right and the double doors leading to the kitchen quarters on the left, past the side door to the terrace and on to the door that gave admission to the Oak suite that had been allotted to Christian Gulbrandsen. It was a room furnished as a sitting-room more than a bedroom, with a bed in an alcove to one side and a door leading into a dressing-room and bathroom.

Carrie Louise stopped on the threshold. Christian Gulbrandsen had been sitting at the big mahogany desk with a small portable typewriter open in front of him. He sat there now, but slumped sideways in the chair. The high arms of the chair prevented him from slipping to the floor.

Lewis Serrocold was standing by the window. He had pulled the curtain a little aside and was gazing out into the night.

He looked round and frowned.

'My dearest, you shouldn't have come.'

He came towards her and she stretched out a hand to him. Miss Marple retreated a step or two.

'Oh yes, Lewis. I had to – see him. One has to know just exactly how things are.'

She walked slowly towards the desk.

Lewis said warningly:

'You mustn't touch anything. The police must have things left exactly as we found them.'

'Of course. He was shot deliberately by someone, then?'

'Oh yes.' Lewis Serrocold looked a little surprised that the question had even been asked. 'I thought – you knew that?'

'I did really. Christian would not commit suicide, and he was such a competent person that it could not possibly have been an accident. That only leaves' – she hesitated a moment – 'murder.'

She walked up behind the desk and stood looking down at the dead man. There was sorrow and affection in her face.

'Dear Christian,' she said. 'He was always good to me.'

Softly, she touched the top of his head with her fingers.

'Bless you and thank you, dear Christian,' she said.

Lewis Serrocold said with something more like emotion than Miss Marple had ever seen in him before:

'I wish to God I could have spared you this, Caroline.'

His wife shook her head gently.

'You can't really spare anyone anything,' she said. 'Things always have to be faced sooner or later. And therefore it had better be sooner. I'll go and lie down now. I suppose you'll stay here, Lewis, until the police come?'

'Yes.'

Carrie Louise turned away and Miss Marple slipped an arm round her.

Chapter 9

I

Inspector Curry and his entourage found Miss Bellever alone in the Great Hall when they arrived.

She came forward efficiently.

'I am Juliet Bellever, companion and secretary to Mrs Serrocold.'

'It was you who found the body and telephoned to us?'

'Yes. Most of the household are in the library – through that door there. Mr Serrocold remained in Mr Gulbrandsen's room to see that nothing was disturbed. Dr Maverick, who first examined the body, will be here very shortly. He had to take a – case over to the other wing. Shall I lead the way?'

'If you please.'

'Competent woman,' thought the Inspector to himself. 'Seems to have got the whole thing taped.'

He followed her along the corridor.

For the next twenty minutes the routine of police procedure was duly set in motion. The photographer took the necessary pictures. The police surgeon arrived and was joined by Dr Maverick. Half an hour later, the ambulance had taken away the mortal remains of Christian Gulbrandsen, and Inspector Curry started his official interrogation.

Lewis Serrocold took him into the library, and he glanced keenly round the assembled people, making brief notes in his mind. An old lady with white hair, a middle-aged lady, the good looking girl he'd seen driving her car round the countryside, that sulky looking American husband of hers. A couple of young men who were mixed up in the outfit somewhere or other and the capable woman, Miss Bellever, who'd phoned him and met him on arrival.

Inspector Curry had already thought out a little speech and he now delivered it as planned.

'I'm afraid this is all very upsetting to you,' he said, 'and I hope not to keep you too long this evening. We can go into things more thoroughly tomorrow. It was Miss Bellever who found Mr Gulbrandsen dead, and I'll ask Miss Bellever to give me an outline of the general situation as that will save too much repetition. Mr Serrocold, if you want to go up to your wife, please do, and when I have finished with Miss Bellever, I should like to talk to you. Is that all quite clear? Perhaps there is some small room where –'

Lewis Serrocold said: 'My office, Jolly?'

Miss Bellever nodded, and said: 'I was just going to suggest it.'

She led the way across the Great Hall, and Inspector Curry and his attendant Sergeant followed her.

Miss Bellever arranged them and herself suitably. It might have been she and not Inspector Curry who was in charge of the investigation.

The moment had come, however, when the initiative passed to him. Inspector Curry had a pleasant voice and manner. He looked quiet and serious and just a little apologetic. Some people made the mistake of underrating him. Actually he was as competent in his way as Miss Bellever was in hers. But he preferred not to make a parade of the fact.

He cleared his throat.

'I've had the main facts from Mr Serrocold. Mr Christian Gulbrandsen was the eldest son of the late Eric Gulbrandsen, the founder of the Gulbrandsen Trust and Fellowships . . . and all the rest of it. He was one of the trustees of this place and he arrived here unexpectedly yesterday. That is correct?'

'Yes.'

Inspector Curry was pleased by her conciseness. He went on:

Agatha Christie

'Mr Serrocold was away in Liverpool. He returned this evening by the 6.30 train.'

'Yes.'

'After dinner this evening, Mr Gulbrandsen announced his intention of working in his own room and left the rest of the party here after coffee had been served. Correct?'

'Yes.'

'Now, Miss Bellever, please tell me in your own words how you came to discover him dead.'

'There was a rather unpleasant incident this evening. A young man, a psychopathic case, became very unbalanced and threatened Mr Serrocold with a revolver. They were locked in this room. The young man eventually fired the revolver – you can see the bullet holes in the wall there. Fortunately Mr Serrocold was unhurt. After firing the shots, this young man went completely to pieces. Mr Serrocold sent me to find Dr Maverick. I got through on the house phone but he was not in his room. I found him with one of his colleagues and gave him the message and he came here at once. On my own way back I went to Mr Gulbrandsen's room. I wanted to ask him if there was anything he would like – hot milk, or whisky, before settling for the night. I knocked, but there was no response, so I opened the door. I saw that Mr Gulbrandsen was dead. I then rang you up.'

'What entrances and exits are there to the house? And how are they secured? Could anyone have come in from outside without being heard or seen?'

'Anyone could have come in by the side door to the terrace. That is not locked until we all go to bed, as people come in and out that way to go to the College buildings.'

'And you have, I believe, between two hundred and two hundred and fifty juvenile delinquents in the College?'

'Yes. But the College buildings are well secured and patrolled. I should say it was most unlikely that anyone could leave the College unsponsored.'

'We shall have to check up on that, of course. Had Mr Gulbrandsen given any cause for – shall we say, rancour? Any unpopular decisions as to policy?'

Miss Bellever shook her head.

'Oh no, Mr Gulbrandsen had nothing whatever to do with the running of the College, or with administrative matters.'

'What was the purpose of his visit?'

'I have no idea.'

'But he was annoyed to find Mr Serrocold absent, and immediately decided to wait until he returned?'

'Yes.'

'So his business here was definitely with Mr Serrocold?'

'Yes. But it would be – because it would be almost certainly business to do with the Institute.'

'Yes, presumably that is so. Did he have a conference with Mr Serrocold?'

'No, there was no time. Mr Serrocold only arrived just before dinner this evening.'

'But after dinner, Mr Gulbrandsen said he had important letters to write and went away to do so. He didn't suggest a session with Mr Serrocold?'

Miss Bellever hesitated.

'No. No, he didn't.'

'Surely that was rather odd – if he had waited on at inconvenience to himself to see Mr Serrocold?'

'Yes, it was odd.'

The oddness of it seemed to strike Miss Bellever for the first time.

'Mr Serrocold did not accompany him to his room?'

'No. Mr Serrocold remained in the Hall.'

'And you have no idea at what time Mr Gulbrandsen was killed?'

'I think it is possible that we heard the shot. If so, it was at twenty-three minutes past nine.'

'You heard a shot? And it did not alarm you?'

'The circumstances were peculiar.'

She explained in rather more detail the scene between Lewis Serrocold and Edgar Lawson which had been in progress.

'So it occurred to no one that the shot might actually have come from within the house?'

'No. No, I certainly don't think so. We were all so relieved, you know, that the shot didn't come from in here.'

Miss Bellever added rather grimly:

'You don't expect murder and attempted murder in the same house on the same night.'

Inspector Curry acknowledged the truth of that.

'All the same,' said Miss Bellever, suddenly, 'you know, I believe that's what made me go along to Mr Gulbrandsen's room later. I did mean to ask him if he would like anything, but it was a kind of excuse to reassure myself that everything was all right.'

Inspector Curry stared at her for a moment.

'What made you think it mightn't be all right?'

'I don't know. I think it was the shot outside. It hadn't meant anything at the time. But afterwards it came back into my mind. I told myself that it was only a backfire from Mr Restarick's car –'

'Mr Restarick's car?'

'Yes. Alex Restarick. He arrived by car this evening – he arrived just after all this happened.'

'I see. When you discovered Mr Gulbrandsen's body, did you touch anything in the room?'

'Of course not.' Miss Bellever sounded reproachful. 'Naturally I knew that nothing must be touched or moved. Mr Gulbrandsen had been shot through the head but there was no firearm to be seen, so I knew it was murder.'

'And just now, when you took us into the room, everything was exactly as it had been when you found the body?'

Miss Bellever considered. She sat back screwing up her eyes. She had Inspector Curry thought, one of those photographic memories.

'One thing was different,' she said. 'There was nothing in the typewriter.'

'You mean,' said Inspector Curry, 'that when you first went in Mr Gulbrandsen had been writing a letter on the typewriter, and that that letter had since been removed?'

'Yes, I'm almost sure that I saw the white edge of the paper sticking up.'

'Thank you, Miss Bellever. Who else went into that room before we arrived?'

'Mr Serrocold, of course. He remained there when I came to meet you. And Mrs Serrocold and Miss Marple went there. Mrs Serrocold insisted.'

'Mrs Serrocold and Miss Marple,' said Inspector Curry. 'Which is Miss Marple?'

'The old lady with white hair. She was a school friend of Mrs Serrocold's. She came on a visit about four days ago.'

'Well, thank you, Miss Bellever. All that you have told us is quite clear. I'll go into things with Mr Serrocold now. Ah, but perhaps – Miss Marple's an old lady, isn't she? I'll just have a word with her first and then she can go off to bed. Rather cruel to keep an old lady like that up,' said Inspector Curry virtuously. 'This must have been a shock to her.'

'I'll tell her, shall I?'

'If you please.'

Miss Bellever went out. Inspector Curry looked at the ceiling.

'Gulbrandsen?' he said. 'Why Gulbrandsen? Two hundred odd maladjusted youngsters on the premises. No reason any of them shouldn't have done it. Probably one of them did. But why Gulbrandsen? The stranger within the gates.'

Sergeant Lake said: 'Of course we don't know everything yet.'

Inspector Curry said:

'So far, we don't know anything at all.'

He jumped up and was gallant when Miss Marple came in. She seemed a little flustered and he hurried to put her at her ease.

'Now don't upset yourself, m'am.' The old ones like M'am, he thought. To them, police officers were definitely of the lower classes and should show respect to their betters. 'This is all very distressing, I know.

But we've just got to get the facts clear. Get it all clear.'

'Oh yes, I know,' said Miss Marple. 'So difficult, isn't it? To be clear about anything, I mean. Because if you're looking at one thing, you can't be looking at another. And one so often looks at the wrong thing, though whether because one happens to do so or because you're meant to, it's very hard to say. Misdirection, the conjurers call it. So clever, aren't they? And I never *have* known how they manage with a bowl of goldfish – because really that cannot fold up small, can it?'

Inspector Curry blinked a little and said soothingly:

'Quite so. Now, m'am, I've had an account of this evening's events from Miss Bellever. A most anxious time for all of you, I'm sure.'

'Yes, indeed. It was all so *dramatic*, you know.'

'First this to-do between Mr Serrocold and' – he looked down at a note he had made – 'this Edgar Lawson.'

'A very odd young man,' said Miss Marple. 'I have felt all along that there was something wrong about him.'

'I'm sure you have,' said Inspector Curry. 'And then, after that excitement was over, there came Mr Gulbrandsen's death. I understand that you went with Mrs Serrocold to see the – er – the body.'

'Yes, I did. She asked me to come with her. We are very old friends.'

'Quite so. And you went along to Mr Gulbrandsen's room. Did you touch anything while you were in the room, either of you?'

'Oh no. Mr Serrocold warned us not to.'

'Did you happen to notice, ma'm, whether there was a letter or a piece of paper, say, in the typewriter?'

'There wasn't,' said Miss Marple promptly. 'I noticed that at once because it seemed to me odd. Mr Gulbrandsen was sitting there at the typewriter so he must have been typing something. Yes, I thought it very odd.'

Inspector Curry looked at her sharply. He said:

'Did you have much conversation with Mr Gulbrandsen while he was here?'

'Very little.'

'There is nothing especial – or significant that you can remember?'

Miss Marple considered.

'He asked me about Mrs Serrocold's health. In particular, about her heart.'

'Her heart? Is there something wrong with her heart?'

'Nothing whatever, I understand.'

Inspector Curry was silent for a moment or two, then he said:

'You heard a shot this evening during the quarrel between Mr Serrocold and Edgar Lawson?'

'I didn't actually hear it myself. I am a little deaf, you know. But Mrs Serrocold mentioned it as being outside in the park.'

'Mr Gulbrandsen left the party immediately after dinner, I understand?'

'Yes, he said he had letters to write.'

'He didn't show any wish for a business conference with Mr Serrocold?'

'No.'

Miss Marple added:

'You see, they'd already had one little talk.'

'They had? When? I understood that Mr Serrocold only returned home just before dinner.'

'That's quite true, but he walked up through the park, and Mr Gulbrandsen went out to meet him and they walked up and down the terrace together.'

'Who else knows this?'

'I shouldn't think anybody else,' said Miss Marple. 'Unless, of course, Mr Serrocold told Mrs Serrocold. I just happened to be looking out of my window – at some birds.'

'Birds?'

'Birds,' Miss Marple added after a moment or two: 'I thought, perhaps, they might be siskins.'

Inspector Curry was uninterested in siskins.

'You didn't,' he said delicately, 'happen to – er – overhear anything of what they said?'

Innocent china blue eyes met his.

'Only fragments, I'm afraid,' said Miss Marple gently.

'And those fragments?'

Miss Marple was silent for a moment, then she said:

'I do not know the actual subject of their conversation, but their immediate concern was to keep whatever it was from the knowledge of Mrs Serrocold. To spare her – that was how Mr Gulbrandsen put it, and Mr Serrocold said, "I agree that it is she who must be considered." They also mentioned a "big responsibility" and that they should, perhaps, "take outside advice."'

She paused.

'I think you know, you had better ask Mr Serrocold himself about all this.'

'We shall do so, m'am. Now there is nothing else that struck you as unusual this evening?'

Miss Marple considered.

'It was all so unusual if you know what I mean –'

'Quite so. Quite so.'

Something flickered into Miss Marple's memory.

'There was one rather unusual incident. Mr Serrocold stopped Mrs Serrocold from taking her medicine. Miss Bellever was quite put out about it.'

She smiled in a deprecating fashion.

'But that, of course, is such a little thing . . .'

'Yes, of course. Well, thank you, Miss Marple.'

As Miss Marple went out of the room, Sergeant Lake said:

'She's old, but she's sharp . . .'

Chapter 10

I

Lewis Serrocold came into the office and immediately the whole focus of the room shifted. He turned to close the door behind him, and in doing so he created an atmosphere of privacy. He walked over and sat down, not in the chair Miss Marple had just vacated, but in his own chair behind the desk. Miss Bellever had settled Inspector Curry in a chair drawn up to one side of the desk, as though unconsciously she had reserved Lewis Serrocold's chair against his coming.

When he had sat down, Lewis Serrocold looked at the two police officers thoughtfully. His face looked drawn and tired. It was the face of a man who was passing through a severe ordeal, and it surprised Inspector Curry a little because, though Christian Gulbrandsen's death must undeniably have been a shock to Lewis Serrocold, yet Gulbrandsen had not been a close friend or relation, only a rather remote connection by marriage.

In an odd way, the tables seemed to have been turned. It did not seem as though Lewis Serrocold had come into the room to answer police questioning. It seemed rather that Lewis Serrocold had arrived to preside over a court of inquiry. It irritated Inspector Curry a little.

He said briskly:

'Now, Mr Serrocold –'

Lewis Serrocold still seemed lost in thought. He said with a sigh: 'How difficult it is to know the right thing to do.'

Inspector Curry said:

'I think *we* will be the judges of that, Mr Serrocold. Now about Mr Gulbrandsen, he arrived unexpectedly, I understand?'

'Quite unexpectedly.'

'You did not know he was coming.'

'I had not the least idea of it.'

'And you have no idea of why he came?'

Lewis Serrocold said quietly:

'Oh yes, I know why he came. He told me.'

'When?'

'I walked up from the station. He was watching from the house and came out to meet me. It was then that he explained what had brought him here.'

'Business connected with the Gulbrandsen Institute, I suppose?'

'Oh no, it was nothing to do with the Gulbrandsen Institute.'

'Miss Bellever seemed to think it was.'

'Naturally. That would be the assumption. Gulbrandsen did nothing to correct that impression. Neither did I.'

'Why, Mr Serrocold?'

Lewis Serrocold said slowly:

'Because it seemed to both of us important that no hint should arise as to the real purpose of his visit.'

'What was the real purpose?'

Lewis Serrocold was silent for a minute or two. He sighed.

'Gulbrandsen came over here regularly twice a year for meetings of the trustees. The last meeting was only a month ago. Consequently he was not due to come over again for another five months. I think, therefore, that anyone might realize that the business that brought him must definitely be urgent business, but I still think that the normal assumption would be that it *was* a business visit, and that the matter, however urgent – would be a Trust matter. As far as I know, Gulbrandsen did nothing to contradict that impression – or thought he didn't. Yes, perhaps that is nearer the truth – he thought he didn't.'

'I'm afraid, Mr Serrocold, that I don't quite follow you.'

Lewis Serrocold did not answer at once. Then he said gravely:

'I fully realize that with Gulbrandsen's death – which was murder, undeniably murder, I have got to put all the facts before you. But frankly, I am concerned for my wife's happiness and peace of mind. It is not for me to dictate to you, Inspector, but if you can see your way to keeping certain things from her as far as possible I shall be grateful. You see, Inspector Curry, Christian Gulbrandsen came here expressly to tell me that he believed my wife was being slowly and cold-bloodedly poisoned.'

'What?'

Curry leaned forward incredulously.

Serrocold nodded.

'Yes, it was, as you can imagine, a tremendous shock to me. I had had no suspicion of such a thing myself, but as soon as Christian told me, I realized that certain symptoms my wife had complained of lately were quite compatible with that belief. What she took to be rheumatism, leg cramps, pain, and occasional sickness. All that fits in very well *with the symptoms of arsenical poisoning.*'

'Miss Marple told us that Christian Gulbrandsen asked her about the condition of Mrs Serrocold's heart.'

'Did he now? That's interesting. I suppose he thought that a heart poison would be used since it paved the way to a sudden death without undue suspicion. But I think myself that arsenic is more likely.'

'You definitely think, then, that Christian Gulbrandsen's suspicions were well founded?'

'Oh yes, I think so. For one thing, Gulbrandsen would hardly come to me with such a suggestion unless he was fairly sure of his facts. He was a cautious and hard-headed man, difficult to convince, but very shrewd.'

'What was his evidence?'

'We had no time to go into that. Our interview was a hurried one. It served only the purpose of explaining his visit, and a mutual agreement that nothing whatever should be said to my wife about the matter until we were sure of our facts.'

'And whom did he suspect of administering poison?'

'He did not say, and actually I don't think he knew. He *may* have suspected. I think now that he probably did suspect – otherwise why should he be killed?'

'But he mentioned no name to you?'

'He mentioned no name. We agreed that we must investigate the matter thoroughly, and he suggested inviting the advice and co-operation of Dr Galbraith, the Bishop of Cromer. Dr Galbraith is a very old friend of the Gulbrandsens and is one of the trustees of the Institute. He is a man of great wisdom and experience and would be of infinite help and comfort to my wife if – if it was necessary to tell her of our suspicions. We meant to rely on his advice as to whether or not to consult the police.'

'Quite extraordinary,' said Curry.

'Gulbrandsen left us after dinner to write to Dr Galbraith. He was actually in the act of typing a letter to him when he was shot.'

'How do you know?'

Lewis said calmly:

'Because I took the letter out of the typewriter. I have it here.'

From his breast pocket, he drew out a folded type-written sheet of paper and handed it to Curry.

The latter said sharply:

'You shouldn't have taken this, or touched anything in the room.'

'I touched nothing else. I know that I committed an unpardonable offence in your eyes in moving this, but I had a very strong reason. I felt certain that my wife would insist on coming into the room and I was afraid that she might read something of what is written here. I admit myself in the wrong, but I am afraid I would

do the same again. I would do anything – *anything* –
to save my wife unhappiness.'

Inspector Curry said no more for the moment. He
read the typewritten sheet.

Dear Dr Galbraith.

If it is at all possible, I beg that you will come to
Stonygates as soon as you receive this. A crisis of
extraordinary gravity has arisen and I am at a loss how
to deal with it. I know how deep your affection is for our
dear Carrie Louise, and how grave your concern will be
for anything that affects her. How much has she got to
know? How much can we keep from her? Those are the
questions that I find difficult to answer.

Not to beat about the bush, I have reason to believe that
that sweet and innocent lady is being slowly poisoned. I
first suspected this when –

Here the letter broke off abruptly.

Curry said:

'And when he had reached this point Christian
Gulbrandsen was shot?'

'Yes.'

'But why on earth was this letter in the typewriter?'

'I can only conceive of two reasons – one, that the
murderer had no idea to whom Gulbrandsen was writing and what was the subject of the letter. Secondly –

137

he may not have had time. He may have heard someone coming and only had just time to escape unobserved.'

'And Gulbrandsen gave you no hint as to whom he suspected – if he did suspect anyone?'

There was, perhaps, a very slight pause before Lewis answered.

'None whatever.'

He added, rather obscurely:

'Christian was a very fair man.'

'How do you think this poison, arsenic or whatever it may be – was or is being administered?'

'I thought over that whilst I was changing for dinner and it seemed to me that the most likely vehicle was some medicine, a tonic, that my wife was taking. As regards food, we all partake of the same dishes and my wife has nothing specially prepared for her. But anyone could add arsenic to the medicine bottle.'

'We must take the medicine and have it analysed.'

Lewis said quietly:

'I already have a sample of it. I took it this evening before dinner.'

From a drawer in the desk he took out a small corked bottle with a red fluid in it.

Inspector Curry said with a curious glance:

'You think of everything, Mr Serrocold.'

'I believe in acting promptly. Tonight, I stopped my wife from taking her usual dose. It is still in a glass on the oak dresser in the Hall – the bottle of tonic itself is in the dining-room.'

Curry leaned forward across the desk. He lowered his voice and spoke confidentially and without official-dom.

'You'll excuse me, Mr Serrocold, but just *why* are you so anxious to keep this from your wife? Are you afraid she'd panic? Surely, for her own sake, it would be as well if she were warned.'

'Yes – yes, that may well be so. But I don't think you quite understand. Without knowing my wife Caroline, it would be difficult. My wife, Inspector Curry, is an idealist, a completely trustful person. Of her it may truly be said that she sees no evil, hears no evil, and speaks no evil. It would be inconceivable to her that anyone could wish to kill her. But we have to go farther than that. It is not just "anyone." It is a case – surely you see that – of someone possibly very near and dear to her . . .'

'So that's what you think?'

'We have got to face facts. Close at hand we have a couple of hundred warped and stunted personalities who have expressed themselves often enough by crude and senseless violence. But by the very nature of things, none of *them* can be suspect in this case. A slow poisoner is someone living in the intimacy of family life. Think of the people who are here in this house; her husband, her daughter, her granddaughter, her granddaughter's husband, her stepson whom she regards as her own son, Miss Bellever her devoted companion and friend of many years. All very near and dear to her – and yet the suspicion must arise – is it one of them?'

Curry said slowly:

'There *are* outsiders –'

'Yes, in a sense. There is Dr Maverick, one or two of the staff are often with us, there are the servants – but frankly, what possible motive could they have?'

Inspector Curry said:

'And there's young – what is his name again – Edgar Lawson?'

'Yes. But he has only been down here as a casual visitor just lately. He has no possible motive. Besides, he is deeply attached to Caroline – just as everyone is.'

'But he's unbalanced. What about this attack on you tonight?'

Serrocold waved it aside impatiently.

'Sheer childishness. He had no intention of harming me.'

'Not with these two bullet holes in the wall? He shot at you, didn't he?'

'He didn't mean to hit me. It was play-acting, no more.'

'Rather a dangerous form of play-acting, Mr Serrocold.'

'You don't understand. You must talk to our psychiatrist, Dr Maverick. Edgar is an illegitimate child. He has consoled himself for his lack of a father and a humble origin by pretending to himself that he is the son of a celebrated man. It's a well-known phenomenon, I assure you. He was improving, improving very much. Then, for some reason, he had a set-back. He identified me as his "father" and made a melodramatic attack, waving a revolver and uttering threats. I was not in the least alarmed. When he had actually fired the revolver, he broke down and sobbed and Dr Maverick took him away and gave him a sedative. He'll probably be quite normal tomorrow morning.'

'You don't wish to bring a charge against him?'

'That would be the worst thing possible – for him, I mean.'

'Frankly, Mr Serrocold, it seems to me he ought to be under restraint. People who go about firing off revolvers to bolster up their egos – ! One has to think of the community, you know.'

'Talk to Dr Maverick on the subject,' urged Lewis. 'He'll give you the professional point of view. In any case,' he added, 'poor Edgar certainly did not shoot Gulbrandsen. He was in here threatening to shoot *me*.'

Agatha Christie

'That's the point I was coming to, Mr Serrocold. We've covered the outside. Anyone, it seems, could have come in from *outside*, and shot Mr Gulbrandsen, since the terrace door was unlocked. But there is a narrower field *inside* the house, and in view of what you have been telling me, it seems to me that very close attention must be paid to that. It seems possible that, with the exception of old Miss – er – yes, Marple, who happened to be looking out of her bedroom window, no one was aware that you and Christian Gulbrandsen had already had a private interview. If so, Gulbrandsen may have been shot to prevent him communicating his suspicions to you. Of course it is too early to say as yet what other motives may exist. Mr Gulbrandsen was a wealthy man, I presume?'

'Yes, he was a very wealthy man. He has sons and daughters and grandchildren – all of them will probably benefit by his death. But I do not think that any of his family are in this country, and they are all solid and highly respectable people. As far as I know, there are no black sheep amongst them.'

'Had he any enemies?'

'I should think it most unlikely. He was – really, he was not that type of man.'

'So it boils down, doesn't it, to this house and the people in it? Who from *inside* the house could have killed him?'

Lewis Serrocold said slowly:

'That is difficult for me to say. There are the servants and the members of my household and our guests. They are, from your point of view, all possibilities, I suppose. I can only tell you that, as far as I know, everyone except the servants was in the Great Hall when Christian left it, and whilst I was there, nobody left it.'

'Nobody at all?'

'I think' – Lewis frowned in an effort of remembrance – 'oh yes. Some of the lights fused – Mr Walter Hudd went to see to it.'

'That's the young American gentleman?'

'Yes – of course I don't know what took place after Edgar and I came in here.'

'And you can't give me anything nearer than that, Mr Serrocold?'

Lewis Serrocold shook his head.

'No, I'm afraid I can't help you. It's – it's all quite inconceivable.'

Inspector Curry sighed. He said: 'Mr Gulbrandsen was shot with a small automatic pistol. Do you know if anyone in the house has such a weapon?'

'I have no idea, I should think it most unlikely.'

Inspector Curry sighed again. He said:

'You can tell the party that they can all go to bed. I'll talk to them tomorrow.'

When Serrocold had left the room, Inspector Curry said to Lake:

'Well – what do you think?'

'Knows – or thinks he knows, who did it,' said Lake.

'Yes. I agree with you. And he doesn't like it a bit . . .'

Chapter 11

I

Gina greeted Miss Marple with a rush as the latter came down to breakfast the next morning.

'The police are here again,' she said. 'They're in the library this time. Wally is absolutely fascinated by them. He can't understand their being so quiet and so remote. I think he's really quite thrilled by the whole thing. I'm not. I hate it. I think it's horrible. Why do you think I'm so upset? Because I'm half Italian?'

'Very possibly. At least perhaps it explains why you don't mind showing what you feel.'

Miss Marple smiled just a little as she said this.

'Jolly's frightfully cross,' said Gina, hanging on Miss Marple's arm and propelling her into the dining-room. 'I think really because the police are in charge and she can't exactly "run" them like she runs everybody else.

'Alex and Stephen,' continued Gina severely, as they

came into the dining-room where the two brothers were finishing their breakfast, 'just don't care.'

'Gina dearest,' said Alex, 'you are most unkind. Good morning, Miss Marple. I care intensely. Except for the fact that I hardly knew your Uncle Christian, I'm far and away the best suspect. You do realize that, I hope.'

'Why?'

'Well, I was driving up to the house at about the right time, it seems. And they've been checking up on things, and it seems that I took too much time between the lodge and the house – time enough, the implication is, to leave the car, run round the house, go in through the side door, shoot Christian and rush out and back to the car again.'

'And what were you really doing?'

'I thought little girls were taught quite young not to ask indelicate questions. Like an idiot, I stood for several minutes taking in the fog effect in the headlights and thinking what I'd use to get that effect on a stage. For my new "Limehouse" ballet.'

'But you can tell them that!'

'Naturally. But you know what policemen are like. They say "thank you" very civilly and write it all down, and you've no idea *what* they are thinking except that one does feel they have rather sceptical minds.'

'It would amuse me to see you in a spot, Alex,' said

Stephen with his thin, rather cruel smile. 'Now, *I*'m quite all right! I never left the Hall last night.'

Gina cried, 'But they couldn't possibly think it was one of *us*!'

Her dark eyes were round and dismayed.

'Don't say it must have been a tramp, dear,' said Alex, helping himself lavishly to marmalade. 'It's so hackneyed.'

Miss Bellever looked in at the door and said:

'Miss Marple, when you have finished your breakfast, will you go to the library?'

'You again,' said Gina. 'Before any of us.'

She seemed a little injured.

'Hi, what was that?' asked Alex.

'Didn't hear anything,' said Stephen.

'It was a pistol shot.'

'They've been firing shots in the room where Uncle Christian was killed,' said Gina. 'I don't know why. And outside too.'

The door opened again and Mildred Strete came in. She was wearing black with some onyx beads.

She murmured good morning without looking at anyone and sat down.

In a hushed voice she said:

'Some tea, please, Gina. Nothing much to eat – just some toast.'

She touched her nose and her eyes delicately with the

handkerchief she held in one hand. Then she raised her eyes and looked in an unseeing way at the two brothers. Stephen and Alex became uncomfortable. Their voices dropped to almost a whisper and presently they got up and left.

Mildred Strete said, whether to the universe or Miss Marple was not quite certain, 'Not even a black tie!'

'I don't suppose,' said Miss Marple apologetically, 'that they knew beforehand that a murder was going to happen.'

Gina made a smothered sound and Mildred Strete looked sharply at her.

'Where's Walter this morning?' she asked.

Gina flushed.

'I don't know. I haven't seen him.'

She sat there uneasily like a guilty child.

Miss Marple got up.

'I'll go to the library now,' she said.

II

Lewis Serrocold was standing by the window in the library.

There was no one else in the room.

He turned as Miss Marple came in and came forward to meet her, taking her hand in his.

148

'I hope,' he said, 'that you are not feeling the worse for the shock. To be at close quarters with what is undoubtedly murder must be a great strain on anyone who has not come in contact with such a thing before.'

Modesty forbade Miss Marple to reply that she was, by now, quite at home with murder. She merely said that life in St Mary Mead was not quite so sheltered as outside people believed.

'Very nasty things go on in a village, I assure you,' she said. 'One has an opportunity of studying things there that one would never have in a town.'

Lewis Serrocold listened indulgently, but with only half an ear.

He said very simply: 'I want your help.'

'But of course, Mr Serrocold.'

'It is a matter that affects my wife – affects Caroline. I think that you are really attached to her?'

'Yes, indeed. Everyone is.'

'That is what I believed. It seems that I am wrong. With the permission of Inspector Curry, I am going to tell you something that no one else as yet knows. Or perhaps I should say what only one person knows.'

Briefly, he told her what he had told Inspector Curry the night before.

Miss Marple looked horrified.

'I can't believe it, Mr Serrocold. I really can't believe it.'

'That is what I felt when Christian Gulbrandsen told me.'

'I should have said that dear Carrie Louise had not got an enemy in the world.'

'It seems incredible that she should have. But you see the implication? Poisoning – slow poisoning – is an intimate family matter. It must be one of our closely-knit little household –'

'If it is *true*. Are you sure that Mr Gulbrandsen was not mistaken?'

'Christian was not mistaken. He is too cautious a man to make such a statement without foundation. Besides, the police took away Caroline's medicine bottle and a separate sample of its contents. There was arsenic in both of them – and arsenic was not pre-scribed. The actual quantitative tests will take longer – but the actual fact of arsenic being present is estab-lished.'

'Then her rheumatism – the difficulty in walking – all that –'

'Yes, leg cramps are typical, I understand. Also, before you came, Caroline has had one or two severe attacks of a gastric nature – I never dreamed until Christian came –'

He broke off. Miss Marple said softly: 'So Ruth was right!'

'Ruth?'

Lewis Serrocold sounded surprised. Miss Marple flushed.

'There is something I have not told you. My coming here was not entirely fortuitous. If you will let me explain – I'm afraid I tell things so badly. Please have patience.'

Lewis Serrocold listened whilst Miss Marple told him of Ruth's unease and urgency.

'Extraordinary,' he commented. 'I had no idea of this.'

'It was all so vague,' said Miss Marple. 'Ruth herself didn't know why she had this feeling. There must be a reason – in my experience there always is – but "something wrong" was as near as she could get.'

Lewis Serrocold said grimly:

'Well, it seems that she was right. Now, Miss Marple, you see how I am placed. Am I to tell Carrie Louise of this?'

Miss Marple said quickly: 'Oh no,' in a distressed voice, and then flushed and stared doubtfully at Lewis. He nodded.

'So you feel as I do? As Christian Gulbrandsen did. Should we feel like that with an ordinary woman?'

'Carrie Louise is *not* an ordinary woman. She lives by her trust, by her belief in human nature – oh dear, I am expressing myself very badly. But I do feel that until we know who –'

'Yes, that is the crux. But you do see, Miss Marple, that there is a risk in saying nothing –'

'And so you want me to – how shall I put it? – watch over her?'

'You see, you are the only person whom I can trust,' said Lewis Serrocold simply. 'Everyone here *seems* devoted. But are they? Now your attachment goes back many years.'

'And also I only arrived a few days ago,' said Miss Marple pertinently.

Lewis Serrocold smiled.

'Exactly.'

'It is a very mercenary question,' said Miss Marple apologetically. 'But who exactly would benefit if dear Carrie Louise were to die?'

'Money!' said Lewis bitterly. 'It always boils down to money, doesn't it?'

'Well, I really think it must be in this case. Because Carrie Louise is a very sweet person with a great deal of charm, and one cannot really imagine anyone disliking her. She couldn't, I mean, have an *enemy*. So then it does boil down, as you put it, to a question of money, because as you don't need me to tell you, Mr Serrocold, people will quite often do anything for money.'

'I suppose so, yes.'

He went on: 'Naturally Inspector Curry has already taken up that point. Mr Gilfoy is coming down from

London today and can give detailed information. Gilfoy, Gilfoy, Jaimes and Gilfoy are a very eminent firm of lawyers. This Gilfoy's father was one of the original trustees, and they drew up both Caroline's will and the original will of Eric Gulbrandsen. I will put it in simple terms for you –'

'Thank you,' said Miss Marple gratefully. 'So mystifying the law, I always think.'

'Eric Gulbrandsen, after endowment of the College and various fellowships and trusts and other charitable bequests, and having settled an equal sum on his daughter Mildred and on his adopted daughter Pippa (Gina's mother), left the remainder of his vast fortune in trust, the income from it to be paid to Caroline for her lifetime.'

'And after her death?'

'After her death it was to be divided equally between Mildred and Pippa – or their children if they themselves had predeceased Caroline.'

'So that in fact it goes to Mrs Strete and to Gina.'

'Yes. Caroline has also quite a considerable fortune of her own – though not in the Gulbrandsen class. Half of this she made over to me four years ago. Of the remaining amount, she left ten thousand pounds to Juliet Bellever, and the rest equally divided between Alex and Stephen Restarick, her two stepsons.'

'Oh dear,' said Miss Marple. 'That's bad. That's very bad.'

'You mean?'

'It means everyone in the house had a financial motive.'

'Yes. And yet, you know, I can't believe that any of these people would do murder. I simply can't . . . Mildred is her daughter – and already quite well provided for. Gina is devoted to her grandmother. She is generous and extravagant, but has no acquisitive feelings. Jolly Bellever is fanatically devoted to Caroline. The two Restaricks care for Caroline as though she were really their mother. They have no money of their own to speak of, but quite a lot of Caroline's income has gone towards financing their enterprises – especially so with Alex. I simply can't believe either of those two would deliberately poison her for the sake of inheriting money at her death. I just can't believe any of it, Miss Marple.'

'There's Gina's husband, isn't there?'

'Yes,' said Lewis gravely. 'There is Gina's husband.'

'You don't really know much about him. And one can't help seeing that he's a very unhappy young man.'

Lewis sighed.

'He hasn't fitted in here – no. He's no interest in or

sympathy for what we're trying to do. But after all, why should he? He's young, crude, and he comes from a country where a man is esteemed by the success he makes of life.'

'Whilst here we are so very fond of failures,' said Miss Marple.

Lewis Serrocold looked at her sharply and suspiciously.

She flushed a little and murmured rather incoherently:

'I think sometimes, you know, one can overdo things the other way . . . I mean the young people with a good heredity, and brought up wisely in a good home – and with grit and pluck and the ability to get on in life – well, they are really, when one comes down to it – the sort of people a country *needs*.'

Lewis frowned and Miss Marple hurried on, getting pinker and pinker and more and more incoherent.

'Not that I don't appreciate – I do indeed – you and Carrie Louise – a really noble work – real compassion – and one should have compassion – because after all it's what people *are* that counts – good and bad luck – and much more expected (and rightly) of the lucky ones. But I do think sometimes one's sense of proportion – oh, I don't mean *you*, Mr Serrocold. Really I don't know *what* I mean – but the English *are* rather odd that way. Even in war, so much prouder of their defeats and their retreats than of their victories. Foreigners never can understand why we're so proud of Dunkirk. It's the sort of thing they'd prefer not to mention themselves. But we always seem to be almost embarrassed by a victory – and treat it as though it weren't quite nice to boast about it. And look at all our poets! The Charge of the Light Brigade, and the little *Revenge* went down in the Spanish Main. It's really a very odd characteristic when you come to think of it!'

Miss Marple drew a fresh breath.

'What I really mean is that everything here must seem rather peculiar to young Walter Hudd.'

'Yes,' Lewis allowed. 'I see your point. And Walter has certainly a fine war record. There's no doubt about his bravery.'

'Not that that helps,' said Miss Marple candidly. 'Because war is one thing, and everyday life is quite another. And actually to commit a murder, I think you do need bravery – or perhaps, more often, just conceit. Yes, conceit.'

'But I would hardly say that Walter Hudd had a sufficient motive.'

'Wouldn't you?' said Miss Marple. 'He hates it here. He wants to get away. He wants to get Gina away. And if it's really money he wants, it would be important for Gina to get all the money before she – er – definitely forms an attachment to someone else.'

'An attachment to someone else,' said Lewis, in an astonished voice.

Miss Marple wondered at the blindness of enthusiastic social reformers.

'That's what I said. Both the Restaricks are in love with her, you know.'

'Oh, I don't think so,' said Lewis absently.

He went on:

'Stephen's invaluable to us – quite invaluable. The way he's got those lads coming along – keen – interested. They gave a splendid show last month. Scenery, costumes, everything. It just shows, as I've always said to Maverick, that it's lack of drama in their lives that leads these boys to crime. To dramatize yourself is a child's natural instinct. Maverick says – ah yes, Maverick –'

Lewis broke off.

'I want Maverick to see Inspector Curry about Edgar. The whole thing is so ridiculous really.'

'What do you really know about Edgar Lawson, Mr Serrocold?'

'Everything,' said Lewis positively. 'Everything, that is, that one needs to know. His background, upbringing – his deep-seated lack of confidence in himself –'

Miss Marple interrupted.

'Couldn't Edgar Lawson have poisoned Mrs Serrocold?' she asked.

'Hardly. He's only been here a few weeks. And anyway, it's ridiculous! Why should Edgar want to poison my wife? What could he possibly gain by doing so?'

'Nothing material, I know. But he might have – some *odd* reason. He *is* odd, you know.'

'You mean unbalanced?'

'I suppose so. No, I don't – not quite. What I mean is, he's all *wrong.*'

It was not a very lucid exposition of what she felt. Lewis Serrocold accepted the words at their face value.

'Yes,' he said with a sigh. 'He's all wrong, poor lad. And he was showing such marked improvement. I can't really understand why he had this sudden set-back . . .'

Miss Marple leaned forward eagerly.

'Yes, that's what I wondered. If –'

She broke off as Inspector Curry came into the room.

Chapter 12

I

Lewis Serrocold went away, and Inspector Curry sat down and gave Miss Marple a rather peculiar smile.

'So Mr Serrocold has been asking you to act as watch dog,' he said.

'Well, yes,' she added apologetically: 'I hope you don't mind –'

'*I* don't mind. I think it's a very good idea. Does Mr Serrocold know just how well qualified you are for the post?'

'I don't quite understand, Inspector.'

'I see. He thinks you're just a very nice elderly lady who was at school with his wife.' He shook his head at her. 'We know you're a bit more than that, Miss Marple, aren't you? Crime is right down your street. Mr Serrocold only knows one aspect of crime – the promising beginners. Makes me a bit sick, sometimes.

Agatha Christie

Daresay I'm wrong and old-fashioned. But there are plenty of good decent lads about, lads who could do with a start in life. But there, honesty has to be its own reward – millionaires don't leave trust funds to help the worthwhile. Well – well, don't pay any attention to me. I'm old-fashioned. I've seen boys – and girls – with everything against them, bad homes, bad luck, every disadvantage, and they've had the grit to win through. That's the kind I shall leave my packet to, if I ever have one. But then, of course, that's what I never shall have. Just my pension and a nice bit of garden.'

He nodded his head at Miss Marple.

'Superintendent Blacker told me about you last night. Said you'd had a lot of experience of the seamy side of human nature. Well now, let's have your point of view. Who's the nigger in the woodpile? The G.I. husband?'

'That,' said Miss Marple, 'would be very convenient for everybody.'

Inspector Curry smiled softly to himself.

'A G.I. pinched my best girl,' he said reminiscently. 'Naturally, I'm prejudiced. His manner doesn't help. Let's have the amateur point of view. Who's been secretly and systematically poisoning Mrs Serrocold?'

'Well,' said Miss Marple judicially, 'one is always inclined, human nature being what it is, to think of the *husband*. Or if it's the other way round, the wife.

That's the first assumption, don't you think, in a poisoning case?'

'I agree with you every time,' said Inspector Curry.

'But really – in this case –' Miss Marple shook her head. 'No, frankly – I can *not* seriously consider Mr Serrocold. Because you see, Inspector, he really *is* devoted to his wife. Naturally he would make a parade of being so – but it isn't a parade. It's very quiet, but it's genuine. He loves his wife, and I'm quite certain that he wouldn't poison her.'

'To say nothing of the fact that he wouldn't have any motive for doing so. She's made over her money to him already.'

'Of course,' said Miss Marple primly, 'there are other reasons for a gentleman wanting his wife out of the way. An attachment to a young woman, for instance. But I really don't see any signs of it in this case. Mr Serrocold does not act as though he had any romantic preoccupation. I'm really afraid,' she sounded quite regretful about it, 'we shall have to wash him out.'

'Regrettable, isn't it?' said the Inspector. He grinned. 'And anyway, he couldn't have killed Gulbrandsen. It seems to me that there's no doubt that the one thing hinges on the other. Whoever is poisoning Mrs Serrocold killed Gulbrandsen to prevent him spilling the beans. What we've got to get at now is who had an opportunity to kill Gulbrandsen last night. And our prize suspect – there's no doubt about it – is young Walter Hudd. It was he who switched on a reading lamp which resulted in a fuse going, thereby giving him the opportunity to leave the Hall and go to the fuse box. The fuse box is in the kitchen passage which opens off from the main corridor. It was during his absence from the Great Hall that the shot was heard. So that's suspect No. 1 perfectly placed for committing the crime.'

'And suspect No. 2?' asked Miss Marple.

'Suspect No. 2 is Alex Restarick, who was alone in his car between the lodge and the house and took too long getting there.'

'Anybody else?' Miss Marple leaned forward eagerly – remembering to add: 'It's very kind of you to tell me all this.'

'It's not kindness,' said Inspector Curry. 'I've got to have your help. You put your finger on the spot when you said "Anybody else?" Because there I've got to depend on *you*. You were there, in the Hall last night, and you can tell me *who left it* . . .'

'Yes – yes, I ought to be able to tell you . . . But can I? You see – the circumstances –'

'You mean that you were all listening to the argument going on behind the door of Mr Serrocold's study.'

Miss Marple nodded vehemently.

'Yes, you see we were all really very frightened. Mr

Lawson looked – he really did – quite demented. Apart from Mrs Serrocold, who seemed quite unaffected, we all feared that he would do a mischief to Mr Serrocold. He was shouting, you know, and saying the most terrible things – we could hear them quite plainly – and what with that and with most of the lights being out – I didn't really notice anything else.'

'You mean that whilst that scene was going on, anybody could have slipped out of the Hall, gone along the corridor, shot Mr Gulbrandsen and slipped back again?'

'I think it would have been possible . . .'

'Could you say definitely that anybody was in the Great Hall the whole time?'

Miss Marple considered.

'I could say that Mrs Serrocold was – because I was watching her. She was sitting quite close to the study door, and she never moved from her seat. It surprised me, you know, that she was able to remain so calm.'

'And the others?'

'Miss Bellever went out – but I think – I am almost sure – that that was *after* the shot. Mrs Strete? I really don't know. She was sitting behind me, you see. Gina was over by the far window. I *think* she remained there the whole time but of course I cannot be sure. Stephen was at the piano. He stopped playing when the quarrel began to get heated –'

'We mustn't be misled by the time you heard the shot,' said Inspector Curry. 'That's a trick that's been done before now, you know. Fake up a shot so as to fix the time of a crime, and fix it wrong. *If* Miss Bellever had cooked up something of that kind (far fetched – but you never know) then she'd leave as she did, openly, after the shot was heard. No, we can't go by the shot. The limits are between when Christian Gulbrandsen left the Hall to the moment when Miss Bellever found him dead, and we can only eliminate those people who were known not to have had opportunity. That gives us Lewis Serrocold and young Edgar Lawson in the study, and Mrs Serrocold in the Hall. It's very unfortunate, of course, that Gulbrandsen should be shot on the same evening that this schemozzle happened between Serrocold and this young Lawson.'

'Just unfortunate, you think?' murmured Miss Marple.

'Oh? What do you think?'

'It occurred to me,' murmured Miss Marple, 'that it might have been *contrived*.'

'So that's your idea?'

'Well, everybody seems to think it very odd that Edgar Lawson should quite suddenly have a relapse, so to speak. He'd got this curious complex, or whatever the term is, about his unknown father. Winston Churchill and Viscount Montgomery – all quite likely in his state of mind. Just any famous man he happened to think of. But suppose somebody puts it into his head that it's Lewis Serrocold who is really his father, that it's Lewis Serrocold who has been persecuting him – that he ought by rights to be the Crown Prince as it were of Stonygates. In his weak mental state he'll accept the idea – work himself up into a frenzy, and sooner or later will make the kind of scene he did make. And what a wonderful cover *that* will be! Everybody will have their attention fixed on the dangerous situation that is developing – especially if somebody has thoughtfully supplied him with a revolver.'

'Hm, yes. Walter Hudd's revolver.'

'Oh yes,' said Miss Marple, 'I'd thought of that. But you know, Walter is uncommunicative and he's certainly sullen and ungracious, but I don't really think he's *stupid*.'

'So you don't think it's Walter?'

'I think everybody would be very relieved if it *was* Walter. That sounds very unkind, but it's because he is an outsider.'

'What about his wife?' asked Inspector Curry. 'Would she be relieved?'

Miss Marple did not answer. She was thinking of Gina and Stephen Restarick standing together as she had seen them on her first day. And she thought of the way Alex Restarick's eyes had gone straight to Gina as he had entered the Hall last night. What was Gina's own attitude?

II

Two hours later Inspector Curry tilted back his chair, stretched himself and sighed.

'Well,' he said, 'we've cleared a good deal of ground.'

Sergeant Lake agreed.

'The servants are out,' he said. 'They were together all through the critical period – those that sleep here. The ones that don't live in had gone home.'

Curry nodded. He was suffering from mental fatigue.

He had interviewed physio-therapists, members of the teaching staff, and what he called to himself the 'two young lags,' whose turn it had been to dine with the family that night. All their stories dovetailed and checked. He could write them off. Their activities and habits were communal. There were no lonely souls among them. Which was useful for the purposes of alibis. Curry had kept Dr Maverick, who was, as far as he could judge, the chief person in charge of the Institute, to the end.

'But we'll have him in now, Lake.'

So the young doctor bustled in, neat and spruce and rather inhuman looking behind his pince-nez.

Maverick confirmed the statements of his staff, and agreed with Curry's findings. There had been no slackness, no loophole in the College impregnability. Christian Gulbrandsen's death could not be laid to the account of the 'young patients,' as Curry almost called them, so hypnotized had he become by the fervent medical atmosphere.

'But patients are exactly what they are, Inspector,' said Dr Maverick with a little smile.

It was a superior smile, and Inspector Curry would not have been human if he had not resented it just a little.

He said professionally:

'Now as regards your own movements, Dr Maverick? Can you give me an account of them?'

'Certainly. I have jotted them down for you with approximate times.'

Dr Maverick had left the Great Hall at fifteen minutes after nine, with Mr Lacy and Dr Baumgarten. They had gone to Dr Baumgarten's rooms, where they had all three remained discussing certain courses of treatment until Miss Bellever had come hurrying in and asked Dr Maverick to go to the Great Hall. That was at approximately half-past nine. He had gone at once to the Hall and had found Edgar Lawson in a state of collapse.

Inspector Curry stirred a little.

'Just a minute, Dr Maverick. Is this young man, in your opinion, definitely a mental case?'

Dr Maverick smiled the superior smile again.

'We are all mental cases, Inspector Curry.'

Tomfool answer, thought the Inspector. He knew quite well *he* wasn't a mental case, whatever Dr Maverick might be!

'Is he responsible for his actions? He knows what he is doing, I suppose?'

'Perfectly.'

'Then when he fired that revolver at Mr Serrocold it was definitely attempted murder.'

'No, no, Inspector Curry. Nothing of *that* kind.'

'Come now, Dr Maverick. I've seen the two bullet holes in the wall. They must have gone dangerously near to Mr Serrocold's head.'

'Perhaps. But Lawson had no intention of killing Mr Serrocold or even of wounding him. He is very fond of Mr Serrocold.'

'It seems a curious way of showing it.'

Dr Maverick smiled again. Inspector Curry found that smile very trying.

'Everything one does is intentional. Every time you, Inspector, forget a name or a face it is because, unconsciously, you *wish* to forget it.'

Inspector Curry looked unbelieving.

'Every time you make a slip of the tongue, that slip

has a meaning. Edgar Lawson was standing a few feet away from Mr Serrocold. He could easily have shot him dead. Instead, he missed him. Why did he miss him? Because he *wanted* to miss him. It is as simple as that. Mr Serrocold was never in any danger – and Mr Serrocold himself was quite aware of that fact. He understood Edgar's gesture for exactly what it was – a gesture of defiance and resentment against a universe that has denied him the simple necessities of a child's life – security and affection.'

'I think I'd like to see this young man.'

'Certainly if you wish. His outburst last night has had a cathartic effect. There is a great improvement today. Mr Serrocold will be very pleased.'

Inspector Curry stared hard at him, but Dr Maverick was serious as always.

Curry sighed.

'Do you have any arsenic?' he asked.

'Arsenic?' The question took Dr Maverick by surprise. It was clearly unexpected. 'What a very curious question. Why arsenic?'

'Just answer the question, please.'

'No, I have no arsenic of any kind in my possession.'

'But you have some drugs?'

'Oh certainly. Sedatives. Morphia – the barbiturates. The usual things.'

'Do you attend Mrs Serrocold?'

'No. Dr Gunter of Market Kimble is the family physician. I hold a medical degree, of course, but I practise purely as a psychiatrist.'

'I see. Well, thank you very much, Dr Maverick.'

As Dr Maverick went out, Inspector Curry murmured to Lake that psychiatrists gave him a pain in the neck.

'We'll get on to the family now,' he said. 'I'll see young Walter Hudd first.'

Walter Hudd's attitude was cautious. He seemed to be studying the police officer with a slightly wary expression. But he was quite co-operative.

There was a good deal of defective wiring in Stonygates – the whole electric system was very old-fashioned. They wouldn't stand for a system like that in the States.

'It was installed, I believe, by the late Mr Gulbrandsen when electric light was a novelty,' said Inspector Curry with a faint smile.

'I'll say so! Sweet old feudal English and never been brought up to date.'

The fuse which controlled most of the lights in the Great Hall had gone, and he had gone out to the fuse-box to see about it. In due course he got it repaired and came back.

'How long were you away?'

'Why that I couldn't say for sure. The fuse-box is in an awkward place. I had to get steps and a candle. I was maybe ten minutes – perhaps a quarter of an hour.'

'Did you hear a shot?'

'Why no, I didn't hear anything like that. There are double doors through to the kitchen quarters and one of them is lined with a kind of felt.'

'I see. And when you came back into the Hall, what did you see?'

'They were all crowded round the door into Mr Serrocold's study. Mrs Strete said that Mr Serrocold had been shot – but actually that wasn't so. Mr Serrocold was quite all right. The boob had missed him.'

'You recognized the revolver?'

'Sure I recognized it! It was mine.'

'When did you see it last?'

'Two or three days ago.'

'Where did you keep it?'

'In the drawer in my room.'

'Who knew that you kept it there?'

'I wouldn't know who knows what in this house.'

'What do you mean by that, Mr Hudd?'

'Aw, they're all nuts!'

'When you came into the Hall, was everybody else there?'

'What d'you mean by everybody?'

'The same people who were there when you went to repair the fuse.'

'Gina was there . . . and the old lady with white hair – and Miss Bellever . . . I didn't notice particularly – but I should say so.'

'Mr Gulbrandsen arrived quite unexpectedly the day before yesterday, did he not?'

'I guess so. It wasn't his usual routine, I understand.'

'Did anyone seem upset by his arrival?'

Walter Hudd took a moment or two before he answered:

'Why no, I wouldn't say so.'

Once more there was a touch of caution in his manner.

'Have you any idea why he came?'

'Their precious Gulbrandsen Trust I suppose. The whole set-up here is crazy.'

'You have these "set-ups" as you call it, in the States.'

'It's one thing to endow a scheme, and another to give it the personal touch as they do here. I had enough of psychiatrists in the Army. This place is stiff with them. Teaching young thugs to make raffia baskets and carve pipe-racks. Kids' games! It's sissy!'

Inspector Curry did not comment on this criticism. Possibly he agreed with it.

He said, eying Walter carefully:

'So you have no idea who could have killed Mr Gulbrandsen?'

'One of the bright boys from the College practising his technique, I'd say.'

'No, Mr Hudd, that's out. The College, in spite of its carefully produced atmosphere of freedom, is none the less a place of detention and is run on those lines. Nobody can run in and out of it after dark and commit murders.'

'I wouldn't put it past them! Well – if you want to fix it nearer home, I'd say your best bet was Alex Restarick.'

'Why do you say that?'

'He had the opportunity. He drove up through the grounds alone in his car.'

'And why should he kill Christian Gulbrandsen?'

Walter shrugged his shoulders.

'I'm a stranger. I don't know the family set-ups. Maybe the old boy had heard something about Alex and was going to spill the beans to the Serrocolds.'

'With what results?'

'They might cut off the dough. He can use dough – uses a good deal of it by all accounts.'

'You mean – in theatrical enterprises?'

'That's what he calls it?'

'Do you suggest it was otherwise?'

Again Walter Hudd shrugged his shoulders.

'I wouldn't know,' he said.

Chapter 13

I

Alex Restarick was voluble. He also gestured with his hands.

'I know, I know! I'm the ideal suspect. I drive down here alone and on the way to the house, I get a creative fit. I can't expect you to understand. How should you?'

'I might,' Curry put in drily, but Alex Restarick swept on.

'It's just one of those things! They come upon you there's no knowing when or how. An effect – an idea – and everything else goes to the winds! I'm producing *Limehouse Nights* next month. Suddenly – last night – the set-up was wonderful . . . *The* perfect lighting. Fog – and the headlights cutting through the fog and being thrown back – and reflecting dimly a tall pile of buildings. Everything helped! The shots – the running footsteps – and the chug-chugging of the electric power engine – could have been a launch on the Thames. And I thought – that's it – but what am I going to use to get just these effects? – and –'

Inspector Curry broke in.

'You heard shots? Where?'

'Out of the fog, Inspector.' Alex waved his hands in the air – plump well-kept hands. 'Out of the fog. That was the wonderful part about it.'

'It didn't occur to you that anything was wrong?'

'Wrong? Why should it?'

'Are shots such a usual occurrence?'

'Ah, I knew you wouldn't understand! The shots fitted into the scene I was creating. I *wanted* shots. Danger – opium – crazy business. What did I care what they were really? Backfires from a lorry on the road? A poacher after rabbits?'

'They snare rabbits mostly round here.'

Alex swept on:

'A child letting off fireworks? I didn't even think about them *as* – shots. I was in Limehouse – or rather at the back of the stalls – looking at Limehouse.'

'How many shots?'

'I don't know,' said Alex petulantly. 'Two or three. Two close together, I do remember that.'

Inspector Curry nodded.

'And the sound of running footsteps, I think you said? Where were they?'

'They came to me out of the fog. Somewhere near the house.'

Inspector Curry said gently:

'That would suggest that the murderer of Christian Gulbrandsen came from *outside*.'

'Of course. Why not? You don't really suggest, do you, that he came from inside the house?'

Still very gently Inspector Curry said:

'We have to think of everything.'

'I suppose so,' said Alex Restarick generously. 'What a soul-destroying job yours must be, Inspector! The details, the times and places, the pettifogging *pettiness* of it. And in the end – what good is it all? Does it bring the wretched Christian Gulbrandsen back to life?'

'There's quite a satisfaction in getting your man, Mr Restarick.'

'The Wild Western touch!'

'Did you know Mr Gulbrandsen well?'

'Not well enough to murder him, Inspector. I had met him, off and on, since I lived here as a boy. He made brief appearances from time to time. One of our captains of industry. The type does not interest me. He has quite a collection, I believe, of Thorwaldsen's statuary –' Alex shuddered. 'That speaks for itself, does it not? My God, these rich men!'

Inspector Curry eyed him meditatively. Then he said: 'Do you take any interest in poisons, Mr Restarick?'

'In poisons? My dear man, he was surely not poisoned first and shot afterwards. That would be too madly detective story.'

'He was not poisoned. But you haven't answered my question.'

'Poison has a certain appeal ... It has not the crudeness of the revolver bullet or the blunt weapon. I have no special knowledge of the subject, if that is what you mean.'

'Have you ever had arsenic in your possession?'

'In sandwiches – after the show? The idea has its allurements. You don't know Rose Glidon? These actresses who think they have a name! No I have never thought of arsenic. One extracts it from weed killer or flypapers, I believe.'

'How often are you down here, Mr Restarick?'

'It varies, Inspector. Sometimes not for several weeks. But I try to get down for weekends whenever I can. I always regard Stonygates as my true home.'

'Mrs Serrocold has encouraged you to do so?'

'What I owe Mrs Serrocold can never be repaid. Sympathy, understanding, affection –'

'And quite a lot of solid cash as well, I believe?'

Alex looked faintly disgusted.

'She treats me as a son, and she has belief in my work.'

'Has she ever spoken to you about her will?'

'Certainly. But may I ask what is the point of all these questions, Inspector? There is nothing wrong with Mrs Serrocold.'

'There had better not be,' said Inspector Curry grimly.

'Now what can you possibly mean by that?'

'If you don't know, so much the better,' said Inspector Curry. 'And if you do – I'm warning you.'

When Alex had gone Sergeant Lake said:

'Pretty bogus, would you say?'

Curry shook his head.

'Difficult to say. He may have genuine creative talent. He may just like living soft and talking big. One doesn't know. Heard running footsteps, did he? I'd be prepared to bet he made that up.'

'For any particular reason?'

'Definitely for a particular reason. We haven't come to it yet, but we will.'

'After all, sir, one of those smart lads may have got out of the College buildings unbeknownst. Probably a few cat burglars amongst them, and if so –'

'That's what we're meant to think. Very convenient. But if that's so, Lake, I'll eat my new soft hat.'

II

'I was at the piano,' said Stephen Restarick. 'I'd been strumming softly when the row blew up. Between Lewis and Edgar.'

'What did you think of it?'

'Well – to tell the truth I didn't really take it seriously. The poor beggar has these fits of venom. He's not really loopy, you know. All this nonsense is a kind of blowing off steam. The truth is, we all get under his skin – particularly Gina, of course.'

'Gina? You mean Mrs Hudd? Why does she get under his skin?'

'Because she's a woman – and a very beautiful woman, and because she thinks he's funny! She's half Italian, you know, and the Italians have that unconscious vein of cruelty. They've no compassion for anyone who's old or ugly, or peculiar in any way. They point with their fingers and jeer. That's what Gina did, metaphorically speaking. She'd no use for young Edgar. He was ridiculous, pompous, and at bottom fundamentally unsure of himself. He wanted to impress, and he only succeeded in looking silly. It wouldn't mean anything to her that the poor fellow suffered a lot.'

'Are you suggesting that Edgar Lawson is in love with Mrs Hudd?' asked Inspector Curry.

Stephen replied cheerfully:

'Oh yes. As a matter of fact we all are, more or less! She likes us that way.'

'Does her husband like it?'

'He takes a dim view. He suffers, too, poor fellow. The thing can't last, you know. Their marriage, I mean. It will break up before long. It was just one of these war affairs.'

'This is all very interesting,' said the Inspector. 'But we're getting away from our subject, which is the murder of Christian Gulbrandsen.'

'Quite,' said Stephen. 'But I can't tell you anything about it. I sat at the piano, and I didn't leave the piano until dear Jolly came in with some rusty old keys and tried to fit one to the lock of the study door.'

'You stayed at the piano. Did you continue to play the piano?'

'A gentle obbligato to the life and death struggle in Lewis's study? No, I stopped playing when the tempo rose. Not that I had any doubts as to the outcome. Lewis has what I can only describe as a dynamic eye. He could easily break up Edgar just by looking at him.'

'Yet Edgar Lawson fired two shots at him.'

Stephen shook his head gently.

'Just putting on an act, that was. Enjoying himself. My dear mother used to do it. She died or ran away

181

with someone when I was four, but I remember her blazing off with a pistol if anything upset her. She did it at a night club once. Made a pattern on the wall. She was an excellent shot. Quite a bit of trouble she caused. She was a Russian dancer, you know.'

'Indeed. Can you tell me, Mr Restarick, who left the Hall yesterday evening whilst you were there – during the relevant time?'

'Wally – to fix the lights. Juliet Bellever to find a key to fit the study door. Nobody else, as far as I know.'

'Would you have noticed if somebody did?'

Stephen considered.

'Probably not. That is, if they just tiptoed out and back again. It was so dark in the Hall – and there was the fight to which we were all listening avidly.'

'Is there anyone you are sure *was* there the whole time?'

'Mrs Serrocold – yes, and Gina. I'd swear to them.'

'Thank you, Mr Restarick.'

Stephen went towards the door. Then he hesitated and came back.

'What's all this,' he said, 'about arsenic?'

'Who mentioned arsenic to you?'

'My brother.'

'Ah – yes.'

Stephen said:

'Has somebody been giving Mrs Serrocold arsenic?'

'Why should you mention Mrs Serrocold?'

'I've read of the symptoms of arsenical poisoning. Peripheral neuritis, isn't it? It would square more or less with what she's been suffering from lately. And then Lewis snatching away her tonic last night. Is *that* what's been going on here?'

'The matter is under investigation,' said Inspector Curry in his most official manner.

'Does she know about it herself?'

'Mr Serrocold was particularly anxious that she should not be – alarmed.'

'Alarmed isn't the right word, Inspector. Mrs Serrocold is never alarmed . . . Is that what lies behind Christian Gulbrandsen's death? Did he find out she was being poisoned – but how could he find out? Anyway, the whole thing seems most improbable. It doesn't make sense.'

'It surprises you very much, does it, Mr Restarick?'

'Yes, indeed. When Alex spoke to me I could hardly believe it.'

'Who, in your opinion, would be likely to administer arsenic to Mrs Serrocold?'

For a moment a grin appeared upon Stephen Restarick's handsome face.

'Not the usual person. You can wash out the husband. Lewis Serrocold's got nothing to gain. And also he worships that woman. He can't bear her to have an ache in her little finger.'

'Who then? Have you any idea?'

'Oh yes. I'd say it was a certainty.'

'Explain, please.'

Stephen shook his head.

'It's a certainty psychologically speaking. Not in any other way. No evidence of any kind. And you probably wouldn't agree.'

Stephen Restarick went out nonchalantly, and Inspector Curry drew cats on the sheet of paper in front of him.

He was thinking three things. A, that Stephen Restarick thought a good deal of himself; B, that Stephen Restarick and his brother presented a united front; and C, that Stephen Restarick was a handsome man where Walter Hudd was a plain one.

He wondered about two other things – what Stephen meant by 'psychologically speaking' and whether Stephen could possibly have seen Gina from his seat at the piano. He rather thought not.

III

Into the Gothic gloom of the library, Gina brought an exotic glow. Even Inspector Curry blinked a little at the radiant young woman who sat down, leaned forward over the table and said expectantly, 'Well?'

Inspector Curry, observing her scarlet shirt and dark green slacks, said drily:

'I see you're not wearing mourning, Mrs Hudd?'

'I haven't got any,' said Gina. 'I know everyone is supposed to have a little black number and wear it with pearls. But I don't. I hate black. I think it's hideous, and only receptionists and housekeepers and people like that ought to wear it. Anyway Christian Gulbrandsen wasn't really a relation. He's my grandmother's stepson.'

'And I suppose you didn't know him very well?'

Gina shook her head.

'He came here three or four times when I was a child, but then in the war I went to America, and I only came back here to live about six months ago.'

'You have definitely come back here to live? You're not just on a visit?'

'I haven't really thought,' said Gina.

'You were in the Great Hall last night, when Mr Gulbrandsen went to his room?'

185

'Yes. He said goodnight and went away. Grandam asked if he had everything he wanted and he said yes – that Jolly had fixed him up fine. Not those words, but that kind of thing. He said he had letters to write.'

'And then?'

Gina described the scene between Lewis and Edgar Lawson. It was the same story that Inspector Curry had by now heard many times, but it took an added colour, a new gusto, under Gina's handling. It became drama.

'It was Wally's revolver,' she said. 'Fancy Edgar's having the guts to go and pinch it out of his room. I'd never have believed he'd have the guts.'

'Were you alarmed when they went into the study and Edgar Lawson locked the door?'

'Oh no,' said Gina, opening her enormous brown eyes very wide. 'I loved it. It was so ham, you know, and so madly theatrical. Everything Edgar does is always ridiculous. One can't take him seriously for a moment.'

'He did fire the revolver, though?'

'Yes. We all thought then that he'd shot Lewis after all.'

'And did you enjoy that?' Inspector Curry could not refrain from asking.

'Oh no, I was terrified, then. Everyone was, except Grandam. She never turned a hair.'

'That seems rather remarkable.'

'Not really. She's that kind of person. Not quite in this world. She's the sort of person who never believes *anything* bad can happen. She's sweet.'

'During all this scene, who was in the Hall?'

'Oh we were all there. Except Uncle Christian, of course.'

'Not *all*, Mrs Hudd. People went in and out.'

'Did they?' asked Gina vaguely.

'Your husband, for instance, went out to fix the lights.'

'Yes. Wally's great at fixing things.'

'During his absence, a shot was heard, I understand. A shot that you all thought came from the Park?'

'I don't remember that ... Oh yes, it was just after the lights had come on again and Wally had come back.'

'Did anyone else leave the Hall?'

'I don't think so. I don't remember.'

'Where were you sitting, Mrs Hudd?'

'Over by the window.'

'Near the door to the library?'

'Yes.'

'Did you yourself leave the Hall at all?'

'Leave? With all the excitement? Of course not.'

Gina sounded scandalized by the idea.

'Where were the others sitting?'

'Mostly round the fireplace, I think. Aunt Mildred was knitting and so was Aunt Jane – Miss Marple, I mean – Grandam was just sitting.'

'And Mr Stephen Restarick?'

'Stephen? He was playing the piano to begin with. I don't know where he went later.'

'And Miss Bellever?'

'Fussing about, as usual. She practically never sits down. She was looking for keys or something.'

She said suddenly:

'What's all this about Grandam's tonic? Did the chemist make a mistake in making it up or something?'

'Why should you think that?'

'Because the bottle's disappeared, and Jolly's been fussing round madly looking for it, in no end of a stew. Alex told her the police had taken it away. Did you?'

Instead of replying to the question, Inspector Curry said:

'Miss Bellever was upset, you say?'

'Oh! Jolly always fusses,' said Gina carelessly. 'She likes fussing. Sometimes I wonder how Grandam can stand it.'

'Just one last question, Mrs Hudd. You've no ideas yourself as to who killed Christian Gulbrandsen and why?'

'One of the queers did it, I should think. The thug

ones are really quite sensible. I mean they only cosh people so as to rob a till or get money or jewellery – not just for fun. But one of the queers – you know, what they call mentally maladjusted – might do it for fun, don't you think? Because I can't see what other reason there could be for killing Uncle Christian except fun, do you? At least I don't mean fun, exactly – but –'

'You can't think of a motive?'

'Yes, that's what I mean,' said Gina gratefully. 'He wasn't robbed or anything, was he?'

'But you know, Mrs Hudd, the College buildings were locked and barred. Nobody could get out from there without a pass.'

'Don't you believe it,' Gina laughed merrily. 'Those boys could get out from anywhere! They've taught me a lot of tricks.'

'She's a lively one,' said Lake when Gina had departed. 'First time I've seen her close to. Lovely figure, hasn't she. Sort of a foreign figure, if you know what I mean.'

Inspector Curry threw him a cold glance. Sergeant Lake said hastily that she was a merry one. 'Seems to have enjoyed it all, as you might say.'

'Whether Stephen Restarick is right or not about her marriage breaking up, I notice that she went out of her way to mention that Walter Hudd was back in the Great Hall before that shot was heard.'

'Which, according to everyone else, isn't so?'

'Exactly.'

'She didn't mention Miss Bellever leaving the Hall to look for keys, either.'

'No,' said the Inspector thoughtfully, 'she didn't . . .'

Chapter 14

I

Mrs Strete fitted into the library very much better than
Gina Hudd had done. There was nothing exotic about
Mrs Strete. She wore black with an onyx brooch, and
she wore a hairnet over carefully arranged grey hair.

She looked, Inspector Curry reflected, exactly as the
relict of a Canon of the Established Church should look
– which was almost odd, because so few people ever did
look like what they really were.

Even the tight line of her lips had an ascetic ecclesiastical flavour. She expressed Christian Endurance, and
possibly Christian Fortitude. But not, Curry thought,
Christian Charity.

Moreover it was clear that Mrs Strete was offended.

'I should have thought that you could have given
me *some* idea of when you would want me, Inspector. I have been forced to sit around waiting all the
morning.'

Agatha Christie

It was, Curry judged, her sense of importance that was hurt. He hastened to pour oil on the troubled waters.

'I'm very sorry, Mrs Strete. Perhaps you don't quite know how we set about these things. We start, you know, with the less important evidence – get it out of the way, so to speak. It's valuable to keep to the last a person on whose judgment we can rely – a good observer – by whom we can check what has been told us up to date.'

Mrs Strete softened visibly.

'Oh I see. I hadn't quite realized . . .'

'Now you're a woman of mature judgment, Mrs Strete. A woman of the world. And then this is your home – you're the daughter of the house, and you can tell me all about the people who are in it.'

'I can certainly do that,' said Mildred Strete.

'So you see that when we come to the question of who killed Christian Gulbrandsen, you can help us a great deal.'

'But is there any question? Isn't it perfectly obvious who killed my brother?'

Inspector Curry leant back in his chair. His hand stroked his small neat moustache.

'Well – we have to be careful,' he said. 'You think it's obvious?'

'Of course. That dreadful American husband of

poor Gina's. He's the only stranger here. We know absolutely nothing about him. He's probably one of these dreadful American gangsters.'

'But that wouldn't quite account for his killing Christian Gulbrandsen, would it? Why should he?'

'Because Christian had found out something about him. That's what he came here for so soon after his last visit.'

'Are you sure of that, Mrs Strete?'

'Again it seems to me quite obvious. He let it be thought his visit was in connection with the Trust – but that's nonsense. He was here for that only a month ago. And nothing of importance has arisen since. So he must have come on some private business. He saw Walter on his last visit, and he may have recognized him – or perhaps made inquiries about him in the States – naturally he has agents all over the world – and found out something really damaging. Gina is a very silly girl. She always has been. It is just like her to marry a man she knows nothing about – she's always been man mad! A man wanted by the police, perhaps, or a man who's already married, or some bad character in the underworld. But my brother Christian wasn't an easy man to deceive. He came here, I'm sure, to settle the whole business. Expose Walter and show him up for what he is. And so, naturally, Walter shot him.'

Inspector Curry, adding some out-sized whiskers to one of the cats on his blotting pad, said:

'Ye – es.'

'Don't you agree with me that that's what *must* have happened?'

'It could be – yes,' admitted the Inspector.

'What other solution could there be? Christian had no enemies. What I can't understand is why you haven't already arrested Walter?'

'Well, you see, Mrs Strete, we have to have evidence.'

'You could probably get that easily enough. If you wired to America –'

'Oh yes, we shall check up on Mr Walter Hudd. You can be sure of that. But until we can prove motive, there's not very much to go upon. There's opportunity, of course –'

'He went out just after Christian, pretending the lights had fused –'

'They did fuse.'

'He could easily arrange that.'

'True.'

'That gave him his excuse. He followed Christian to his room, shot him and then repaired the fuse and came back to the Hall.'

'His wife says he came back before you heard the shot from outside.'

'Not a bit of it! Gina would say anything. The Italians are never truthful. And she's a Roman Catholic, of course.'

Inspector Curry side-stepped the ecclesiastical angle.

'You think his wife was in it with him?'

Mildred Strete hesitated for a moment.

'No – no, I don't think that.' She seemed rather disappointed not to think so. She went on: 'That must have been partly the motive – to prevent Gina's learning the truth about him. After all, Gina is his bread and butter.'

'And a very beautiful girl.'

'Oh yes. I've always said Gina is good looking. A very common type in Italy, of course. But if you ask me, it's *money* that Walter Hudd is after. That's why he came over here and has settled down living on the Serrocolds.'

'Mrs Hudd is very well off, I understand?'

'Not at present. My father settled the same sum on Gina's mother as he did on me. But of course she took her husband's nationality (I believe the law is altered now) and what with the war and his being a Fascist, Gina has very little of her own. My mother spoils her, and her American aunt, Mrs Van Rydock, spent fabulous sums on her and bought her everything she wanted during the war years. Nevertheless, from Walter's point of view, he can't lay his hands on much until my mother's death, when a very large fortune will come to Gina.'

'And to you, Mrs Strete.'

A faint colour came into Mildred Strete's cheek.

'And to me, as you say. My husband and myself always lived quietly. He spent very little money except on books – he was a great scholar. My own money has almost doubled itself. It is more than enough for my simple needs. Still one can always use money for the benefit of others. Any money that comes to me, I shall regard as a sacred trust.'

'But it won't be in a Trust, will it?' said Curry, wilfully misunderstanding. 'It will come to you absolutely.'

'Oh yes – in that sense. Yes, it will be mine absolutely.'

Something in the ring of that last word made Inspector Curry raise his head sharply. Mrs Strete was not looking at him. Her eyes were shining, and her long thin mouth was curved in a triumphant smile.

Inspector said in a considering voice:

'So in your view – and of course you've had ample opportunities of judging – Master Walter Hudd wants the money that will come to his wife when Mrs Serrocold dies. By the way, she's not very strong, is she, Mrs Strete?'

'My mother has always been delicate.'

'Quite so. But delicate people often live as long or longer than people who have robust health.'

'Yes, I suppose they do.'

'You haven't noticed your mother's health failing just lately?'

'She suffers from rheumatism. But then one must have something as one grows older. I've no sympathy with people who make a fuss over inevitable aches and pains.'

'Does Mrs Serrocold make a fuss?'

Mildred Strete was silent for a moment. She said at last:

'She does not make a fuss herself, but she is used to being made a fuss of. My stepfather is far too solicitous. And as for Miss Bellever, she makes herself positively ridiculous. In any case, Miss Bellever has had a very bad influence in this house. She came here many years ago, and her devotion to my mother, though admirable in itself, has really become somewhat of an infliction. She literally tyrannizes over my mother. She runs the whole house and takes far too much upon herself. I think it annoys Lewis sometimes. I should never be surprised if he told her to go. She has no tact – no tact whatever, and it is trying for a man to find his wife completely dominated by a bossy woman.'

Inspector Curry nodded his head gently.

'I see . . . I see . . .'

He watched her speculatively.

'There's one thing I don't quite get, Mrs Strete. The position of the two Restarick brothers?'

'More foolish sentiment. Their father married my poor mother for her money. Two years afterwards he ran away with a Jugoslavian singer of the lowest morals. He was a very unworthy person. My mother was soft-hearted enough to be sorry for these two boys. Since it was out of the question for them to spend their holidays with a woman of such notorious morals, she more or less adopted them. They have been hangers-on here ever since. Oh yes, we've plenty of spongers in this house, I can tell you that.'

'Alex Restarick had an opportunity of killing Christian Gulbrandsen. He was in his car alone – driving from the Lodge to the house – what about Stephen?'

'Stephen was in the Hall with us. I don't approve of Alex Restarick – he is getting to look very coarse, and I imagine he leads an irregular life – but I don't really see him as a murderer. Besides, why should he kill my brother?'

'That's what we always come back to, isn't it?' said Inspector Curry genially. 'What did Christian Gulbrandsen know – about someone – that made it necessary for that someone to kill him?'

'Exactly,' said Mrs Strete triumphantly. 'It *must* be Walter Hudd.'

'Unless it's someone nearer home.'

Mildred said sharply:

'What did you mean by that?'

Inspector Curry said slowly:

'Mr Gulbrandsen seemed very concerned about Mrs Serrocold's health whilst he was here.'

Mrs Strete frowned.

'Men always fuss over mother because she looks fragile. I think she likes them to! Or else Christian had been listening to Juliet Bellever.'

'You're not worried about your mother's health yourself, Mrs Strete?'

'No. I hope I'm sensible. Naturally mother is not young –'

'And death comes to all of us,' said Inspector Curry. 'But not ahead of its appointed time. That's what we have to prevent.'

He spoke meaningly. Mildred Strete flared into sudden animation.

'Oh it's wicked – wicked. No one else here really seems to care. Why should they? I'm the only person who was a blood relation to Christian. To mother, he was only a grown-up stepson. To Gina, he isn't really any relation at all. But he was my own brother.'

'Half-brother,' suggested Inspector Curry.

'Half-brother, yes. But we were both Gulbrandsens in spite of the difference in age.'

Curry said gently:

'Yes – yes, I see your point . . .'

Tears in her eyes, Mildred Strete marched out. Curry looked at Lake.

'So she's quite sure it's Walter Hudd,' he said. 'Won't entertain for a moment the idea of its being anybody else.'

'And she may be right.'

'She certainly may. Wally fits. Opportunity – and motive. Because if he wants money quick, his wife's mother would have to die. So Wally tampers with her tonic, and Christian Gulbrandsen sees him do it – or hears about it in some way. Yes, it fits very nicely.'

He paused and said:

'By the way, Mildred Strete likes money . . . She mayn't spend it, but she likes it. I'm not sure why . . . She may be a miser – with a miser's passion. Or she may like the power that money gives. Money for benevolence, perhaps? She's a Gulbrandsen. She may want to emulate Father.'

'Complex, isn't it?' said Sergeant Lake, and scratched his head.

Inspector Curry said:

'We'd better see this screwy young man Lawson, and after that we'll go to the Great Hall and work out who was where – and if – and why – and when . . .

We've heard one or two rather interesting things this morning.'

II

It was very difficult, Inspector Curry thought, to get a true estimate of someone from what other people said.

Edgar Lawson had been described by a good many different people that morning, but looking at him now, Curry's own impressions were almost ludicrously different.

Edgar did not impress him as 'queer' or 'dangerous,' or 'arrogant' or even as 'abnormal.' He seemed a very ordinary young man, very much cast down and in a state of humility approaching that of Uriah Heep's. He looked young and slightly common and rather pathetic.

He was only too anxious to talk and to apologize.

'I know I've done very wrong. I don't know what came over me – really I don't. Making that scene and kicking up such a row. And actually shooting off a pistol. At Mr Serrocold too, who's been so good to me and so patient, too.'

He twisted his hands nervously. They were rather pathetic hands, with bony wrists.

'If I've got to be had up for it, I'll come with you at once. I deserve it. I'll plead guilty.'

Agatha Christie

'No charge has been made against you,' said Inspector Curry crisply. 'So we've no evidence on which to act. According to Mr Serrocold, letting off the pistol was an accident.'

'That's because he's so good. There never was a man as good as Mr Serrocold! He's done everything for me. And I go and repay him by acting like this.'

'What made you act as you did?'

Edgar looked embarrassed.

'I made a fool of myself.'

Inspector Curry said drily:

'So it seems. You told Mr Serrocold in the presence of witnesses that you had discovered that he was your father. Was that true?'

'No, it wasn't.'

'What put that idea into your head? Did someone suggest it to you?'

'Well, it's a bit hard to explain.'

Inspector Curry looked at him thoughtfully, then said in a kindly voice:

'Suppose you try. *We* don't want to make things hard for you.'

'Well, you see, I had a rather hard time of it as a kid. The other boys jeered at me. Because I hadn't got a father. Said I was a little bastard – which I was, of course. Mum was usually drunk and she had men coming in all the time. My father was a foreign seaman,

I believe. The house was always filthy, and it was all pretty fair hell. And then I got to thinking, supposing my Dad had been not just some foreign sailor, but someone important – and I used to make up a thing or two. Kid stuff first – changed at birth – really the rightful heir – that sort of thing. And then I went to a new school and I tried it on once or twice hinting things. Said my father was really an Admiral in the Navy. I got to believing it myself. I didn't feel so bad then.'

He paused and then went on:

'And then – later – I thought up some other ideas. I used to stay at hotels and told a lot of silly stories about being a fighter pilot – or about being in Military Intelligence. I got all sort of mixed up. I didn't seem able to stop telling lies.

'Only I didn't really try to get money by it. It was just swank so as to make people think a bit more of me. I didn't want to be dishonest. Mr Serrocold will tell you – and Dr Maverick – they've got all the stuff about it.'

Inspector Curry nodded. He had already studied Edgar's case history and his police record.

'Mr Serrocold got me clear in the end and brought me down here. He said he needed a secretary to help him – and I did help him! I really did. Only the others laughed at me. They were always laughing at me.'

'What others? Mrs Serrocold?'

'No, not Mrs Serrocold. She's a lady – she's always gentle and kind. No, but Gina treated me like dirt. And Stephen Restarick. And Mrs Strete looked down on me for not being a gentleman. So did Miss Bellever – and what's she? She's a paid companion, isn't she?'

Curry noted the signs of rising excitement.

'So you didn't find them very sympathetic?'

Edgar said passionately:

'It was because of me being a bastard. If I'd had a proper father they wouldn't have gone on like that.'

'So you appropriated a couple of famous fathers?'

Edgar blushed.

'I always seem to get to telling lies,' he muttered.

'And finally you said Mr Serrocold was your father. Why?'

'Because that would stop them once and for all, wouldn't it? If *he* was my father they couldn't do anything to me.'

'Yes. But you accused him of being your enemy – of persecuting you.'

'I know –' He rubbed his forehead. 'I got things all wrong. There are times when I don't – when I don't get things quite right. I get muddled.'

'And you took the revolver from Mr Walter Hudd's room?'

Edgar looked puzzled.

'Did I? Is that where I got it?'

'Don't you remember where you got it?'

Edgar said:

'I meant to threaten Mr Serrocold with it. I meant to frighten him. It was kid stuff all over again.'

Inspector Curry said patiently:

'How did you get the revolver?'

'You just said – out of Walter's room.'

'You remember doing that now?'

'I must have got it from his room. I couldn't have got hold of it any other way, could I?'

'I don't know,' said Inspector Curry. 'Somebody – might have given it to you?'

Edgar was silent – his face a blank.

'Is that how it happened?'

Edgar said passionately:

'I don't remember. I was so worked up. I walked about the garden in a red mist of rage. I thought people were spying on me, watching me, trying to hound me down. Even that nice white-haired old lady . . . I can't understand it all now. I feel I must have been mad. I don't remember where I was and what I was doing half the time!'

'Surely you remember who told you Mr Serrocold was your father?'

Edgar gave the same blank stare.

'Nobody told me,' he said sullenly. 'It just came to me.'

Inspector Curry sighed. He was not satisfied. But he judged he could make no further progress at present.

'Well, watch your step in future,' he said.

'Yes, sir. Yes indeed I will.'

As Edgar went, Inspector Curry slowly shook his head.

'These pathological cases are the devil!'

'D'you think he's mad, sir?'

'Much less mad than I'd imagined. Weak-headed, boastful, a liar – yet a certain pleasant simplicity about him. Highly suggestible I should imagine . . .'

'You think someone did suggest things to him?'

'Oh yes, old Miss Marple was right there. She's a shrewd old bird. But I wish I knew who it was. He won't tell. If we only knew that . . . Come on, Lake, let's have a thorough reconstruction of the scene in the Hall.'

III

'That fixes it pretty well.'

Inspector Curry was sitting at the piano. Sergeant Lake was in a chair by the window overlooking the lake.

Curry went on:

'If I'm half-turned on the piano stool, watching the study door, I can't see you.'

Sergeant Lake rose softly and edged quietly through the door to the library.

'All this side of the room was dark. The only lights that were on were the ones beside the study door. No, Lake, I didn't see you go. Once in the library, you could go out through the other door to the corridor – two minutes to run along to the oak suite, shoot Gulbrandsen and come back through the library to your chair by the window.

'The women by the fire have their backs to you. Mrs Serrocold was sitting *here* – on the right of the fireplace, near the study door. Everyone agrees she didn't move and she's the only one who's in the line of direct vision. Miss Marple was here. She was looking past Mrs Serrocold to the study. Mrs Strete was on the left of the fireplace – close to the door out of the Hall to the lobby, and it's a very dark corner. She *could* have gone and come back. Yes, it's possible.'

Curry grinned suddenly.

'And I could go.' He slipped off the music stool and sidled along the wall and out through the door. 'The only person who might notice I wasn't still at the piano would be Gina Hudd. And you remember what Gina said: "Stephen was at the piano to begin with. *I don't know where he was later.*"'

'So you think it's Stephen?'

'I don't know who it is,' said Curry. 'It wasn't

Edgar Lawson or Lewis Serrocold or Mrs Serrocold or Miss Jane Marple. But for the rest –' He sighed. 'It's probably the American. Those fused lights were a bit too convenient – a coincidence. And yet, you know, I rather like the chap. Still, that isn't evidence.'

He peered thoughtfully at some music on the side of the piano. 'Hindemith? Who's he? Never heard of him. Shostakovitch! What names these people have.' He got up and then looked down at the old-fashioned music stool. He lifted the top of it.

'Here's the old-fashioned stuff. Handel's Largo, Czerny's Exercises. Dates back to old Gulbrandsen, most of this. "I know a lovely Garden" – Vicar's wife used to sing that when I was a boy –'

He stopped – the yellow pages of the song in his hand. Beneath them, reposing on Chopin's Preludes, was a small automatic pistol.

'Stephen Restarick,' exclaimed Sergeant Lake joyfully.

'Now don't jump to conclusions,' Inspector Curry warned him. 'Ten to one that's what we're meant to think.'

Chapter 15

I

Miss Marple climbed the stairs and tapped on the door of Mrs Serrocold's bedroom.

'May I come in, Carrie Louise?'

'Of course, Jane dear.'

Carrie Louise was sitting in front of the dressing table, brushing her silvery hair. She turned her head over her shoulder.

'Is it the police? I'll be ready in a few minutes.'

'Are you all right?'

'Yes, of course. Jolly insisted on my having my breakfast in bed. And Gina came into the room with it on tiptoe as though I might be at death's door! I don't think people realize that tragedies like Christian's death are much less shock to someone old. Because one knows by then how anything may happen – and how little anything really matters that happens in this world.'

'Ye – es,' said Miss Marple dubiously.

'Don't you feel the same, Jane? I should have thought you would.'

Miss Marple said slowly:

'Christian was murdered.'

'Yes . . . I see what you mean. You think that *does* matter?'

'Don't you?'

'Not to Christian,' said Carrie Louise simply. 'It matters, of course, to whoever murdered him.'

'Have you any idea who murdered him?'

Mrs Serrocold shook her head in a bewildered fashion.

'No, I've absolutely no idea. I can't even think of a reason. It must have been something to do with his being here before – just over a month ago. Because otherwise I don't think he would have come here suddenly again for no particular reason. Whatever it was must have started off then. I've thought and I've thought, but I can't remember anything unusual.'

'Oh! The same people who are here now – yes, Alex was down from London about then. And – oh yes, Ruth was here.'

'Ruth?'

'Her usual flying visit.'

'Ruth,' said Miss Marple again. Her mind was active. Christian Gulbrandsen and Ruth? Ruth had come away worried and apprehensive, but had not known why. Something was wrong was all that Ruth could say. Christian Gulbrandsen had known or suspected something that Ruth did not. He had known or suspected that someone was trying to poison Carrie Louise. How had Christian Gulbrandsen come to entertain those suspicions? What had he seen or heard? Was it something that Ruth also had seen or heard but which she had failed to appreciate at its rightful significance? Miss Marple wished that she knew what it could possibly have been. Her own vague hunch that it (whatever it was) had to do with Edgar Lawson seemed unlikely since Ruth had not mentioned him.

She sighed.

'You're all keeping something from me, aren't you?' asked Carrie Louise.

Miss Marple jumped a little as the quiet voice spoke.

'Why do you say that?'

'Because you are. Not Jolly. But everyone else. Even Lewis. He came in while I was having my breakfast, and he acted very oddly. He drank some of my coffee and even had a bit of toast and marmalade. That's so unlike him, because he always has tea and he doesn't like marmalade, so he must have been thinking of something else – and I suppose he must have forgotten to have his own breakfast. He does forget things like meals, and he looked so concerned and preoccupied.'

'Murder –' began Miss Marple.

Carrie Louise said quickly:

'Oh I know. It's a terrible thing. I've never been mixed up in it before. You have, haven't you, Jane?'

'Well – yes – actually I have,' Miss Marple admitted.

'So Ruth told me.'

'Did she tell you that last time she was down here?' asked Miss Marple curiously.

'No, I don't think it was then. I can't really remember.'

Carrie Louise spoke vaguely, almost absent-mindedly.

'What are you thinking about, Carrie Louise?'

Mrs Serrocold smiled and seemed to come back from a long way away.

'I was thinking of Gina,' she said. 'And of what you said about Stephen Restarick. Gina's a dear girl, you know, and she does really love Wally. I'm sure she does.'

Miss Marple said nothing.

'Girls like Gina like to kick up their heels a bit.' Mrs Serrocold spoke in an almost pleading voice. 'They're young and they like to feel their power. It's natural, really. I know Wally Hudd isn't the sort of man we imagined Gina marrying. Normally she'd never have met him. But she did meet him, and fell in love with him – and presumably she knows her own business best.'

'Probably she does,' said Miss Marple.

'But it's so very important that Gina should be happy.'

Miss Marple looked curiously at her friend.

'It's important, I suppose, that everyone should be happy.'

'Oh yes. But Gina's a very special case. When we took her mother – when we took Pippa – we felt that it was an experiment that had simply got to succeed. You see, Pippa's mother –'

Carrie Louise paused.

Miss Marple said:

'Who was Pippa's mother?'

Carrie Louise said: 'Eric and I agreed that we should never tell anybody that. She never knew herself.'

'I'd like to know,' said Miss Marple.

Mrs Serrocold looked at her doubtfully.

'It isn't just curiosity,' said Miss Marple. 'I really – well – *need* to know. I can hold my tongue, you know.'

'You could always keep a secret, Jane,' said Carrie Louise with a reminiscent smile. 'Dr Galbraith – he's the Bishop of Cromer now – he knows. But no one else. Pippa's mother was Katherine Elsworth.'

'Elsworth? Wasn't that the woman who administered arsenic to her husband? Rather a celebrated case.'

'Yes.'

'She was hanged?'

'Yes. But you know it's not at all sure that she did it. The husband was an arsenic eater – they didn't understand so much about those things then.'

'She soaked flypapers.'

'The maid's evidence, we always thought, was definitely malicious.'

'And Pippa was her daughter?'

'Yes. Eric and I determined to give the child a fresh start in life – with love and care and all the things a child needs. We succeeded. Pippa was – herself. The sweetest, happiest creature imaginable.'

Miss Marple was silent a long time.

Carrie Louise turned away from the dressing table.

'I'm ready now. Perhaps you'll ask the Inspector or whatever he is to come up to my sitting-room. He won't mind, I'm sure.'

II

Inspector Curry did not mind. In fact he rather welcomed the chance of seeing Mrs Serrocold on her own territory.

As he stood there waiting for her, he looked round him curiously. It was not his idea of what he termed to himself 'a rich woman's boudoir.'

It had an old-fashioned couch and some rather uncomfortable looking Victorian chairs with twisted woodwork backs. The chintzes were old and faded but of an attractive pattern displaying the Crystal Palace. It was one of the smaller rooms, though even then it was larger than the drawing-room of most modern houses. But it had a cosy rather crowded appearance with its little tables, its bric-à-brac, and its photographs. Curry looked at an old snapshot of two little girls, one dark and lively, the other plain and staring out sulkily on the world from under a heavy fringe. He had seen that same expression that morning. 'Pippa and Mildred' was written on the photograph. There was a photograph of Eric Gulbrandsen hanging on the wall, with a gold mount and a heavy ebony frame. Curry had just found a photograph of a good-looking man with eyes crinkling with laughter who he presumed was John Restarick when the door opened and Mrs Serrocold came in.

She wore black, a floating and diaphanous black. Her little pink and white face looked unusually small under its crown of silvery hair, and there was a frailness about her that caught sharply at Inspector Curry's heart. He understood at that moment a good deal that had perplexed him earlier in the morning. He understood why people were so anxious to spare Caroline Louise Serrocold everything that could be spared her.

And yet, he thought, she isn't the kind that would ever make a fuss . . .

She greeted him, asked him to sit down, and took a chair near him. It was less he who put her at her ease than she who put him at his. He started to ask his questions and she answered them readily and without hesitation. The failure of the lights, the quarrel between Edgar Lawson and her husband, the shot they had heard . . .

'It did not seem to you that the shot was in the house?'

'No, I thought it came from outside. I thought it might have been the backfire of a car.'

'During the quarrel between your husband and this young fellow Lawson in the study, did you notice anybody leaving the Hall?'

'Wally had already gone to see about the lights. Miss Bellever went out shortly afterwards – to get something, but I can't remember what.'

'Who else left the Hall?'

'Nobody, so far as I know.'

'Would you know, Mrs Serrocold?'

She reflected a moment.

'No, I don't think I should.'

'You were completely absorbed in what you could hear going on in the study?'

'Yes.'

'And you were apprehensive as to what might happen there?'

'No – no, I wouldn't say that. I didn't think anything would really happen.'

'But Lawson had a revolver?'

'Yes.'

'And was threatening your husband with it?'

'Yes. But he didn't mean it.'

Inspector Curry felt his usual slight exasperation at this statement. So she was another of them!

'You can't possibly have been sure of that, Mrs Serrocold.'

'Well, but I was sure. In my own mind, I mean. What is it the young people say – putting on an act? That's what I felt it was. Edgar's only a boy. He was being melodramatic and silly and fancying himself as a bold desperate character. Seeing himself as the wronged hero in a romantic story. I was quite sure he would never fire that revolver.'

'But he did fire it, Mrs Serrocold.'

Carrie Louise smiled.

'I expect it went off by accident.'

Again exasperation mounted in Inspector Curry.

'It was not an accident. Lawson fired that revolver twice – and fired it at your husband. The bullets only just missed him.'

Carrie Louise looked startled and then grave.

'I can't really believe that. Oh yes' – she hurried on to forestall the Inspector's protest – 'of course I have to believe it if you tell me so. But I still feel there must be a simple explanation. Perhaps Dr Maverick can explain it to me.'

'Oh yes, Dr Maverick will explain it all right,' said Curry grimly. 'Dr Maverick can explain anything. I'm sure of that.'

Unexpectedly Mrs Serrocold said:

'I know that a lot of what we do here seems to you foolish and pointless, and psychiatrists can be very irritating sometimes. But we *do* achieve results, you know. We have our failures, but we have successes too. And what we try to do is *worth* doing. And though you probably won't believe it, Edgar is really devoted to my husband. He started this silly business about Lewis's being his father because he wants so much to have a father like Lewis. But what I can't understand is why he should suddenly get *violent*. He had been so very much better – really practically normal. Indeed he has always seemed normal to me.'

The Inspector did not argue the point.

He said: 'The revolver that Edgar Lawson had was one belonging to your granddaughter's husband. Presumably Lawson took it from Walter Hudd's room. Now tell me, have you ever seen *this* weapon before?'

On the palm of his hand he held out the small black automatic.

Carrie Louise looked at it.

'No, I don't think so.'

'I found it in the piano stool. It has recently been fired. We haven't had time to check on it fully yet, but I should say that it is almost certainly the weapon with which Mr Gulbrandsen was shot.'

She frowned.

'And you found it in the piano stool?'

'Under some very old music. Music that I should say had not been played for years.'

'Hidden, then?'

'Yes. You remember who was at the piano last night?'

'Stephen Restarick.'

'He was playing?'

'Yes. Just softly. A funny melancholy little tune.'

'When did he stop playing, Mrs Serrocold?'

'When did he stop? I don't know.'

'But he did stop? He didn't go on playing all through the quarrel.'

'No. The music just died down.'

'Did he get up from the piano stool?'

'I don't know. I've no idea what he did until he came over to the study door to try and fit a key to it.'

'Can you think of any reason why Stephen Restarick should shoot Mr Gulbrandsen?'

'None whatever.' She added thoughtfully, 'I don't believe he did.'

'Gulbrandsen might have found out something discreditable about him.'

'That seems to me very unlikely.'

Inspector Curry had a wild wish to reply:

'Pigs may fly but they're very unlikely birds.' It had been a saying of his grandmother's. Miss Marple, he thought, was sure to know it.

III

Carrie Louise came down the broad stairway and three people converged upon her from different directions, Gina from the long corridor, Miss Marple from the library, and Juliet Bellever from the Great Hall.

Gina spoke first.

'Darling!' she exclaimed passionately. 'Are you all right? They haven't bullied you or given you third degree or anything?'

'Of course not, Gina. What odd ideas you have! Inspector Curry was charming and most considerate.'

'So he ought to be,' said Miss Bellever. 'Now, Carrie,

I've got all your letters here and a parcel. I was going to bring them up to you.'

'Bring them into the library,' said Carrie Louise.

All four of them went into the library.

Carrie Louise sat down and began opening her letters. There were about twenty or thirty of them.

As she opened them, she handed them to Miss Bellever, who sorted them into heaps, explaining to Miss Marple as she did so:

'Three main categories. One – from relations of the boys. Those I hand over to Dr Maverick. Begging letters I deal with myself. And the rest are personal – and Cara gives me notes on how to deal with them.'

The correspondence once disposed of, Mrs Serrocold turned her attention to the parcel, cutting the string with scissors.

Out of the neat wrappings there appeared an attractive box of chocolates tied up with gold ribbon.

'Someone must think it's my birthday,' said Mrs Serrocold with a smile.

She slipped off the ribbon and opened the box. Inside was a visiting card. Carrie Louise looked at it with slight surprise.

'*With love from Alex*,' she said. 'How odd of him to send me a box of chocolates by post on the same day he was coming down here.'

Uneasiness stirred in Miss Marple's mind.

She said quickly:

'Wait a minute, Carrie Louise. Don't eat one yet.'

Mrs Serrocold looked faintly surprised.

'I was going to hand them round.'

'Well, don't. Wait while I ask – Is Alex about the house, do you know, Gina?'

Gina said quickly: 'Alex was in the Hall just now, I think.'

She went across, opened the door, and called him.

Alex Restarick appeared in the doorway a moment later.

'Madonna darling! So you're up. None the worse?'

He came across to Mrs Serrocold and kissed her gently on both cheeks.

Miss Marple said:

'Carrie Louise wants to thank you for the chocolates.'

Alex looked surprised.

'What chocolates?'

'These chocolates,' said Carrie Louise.

'But I never sent you any chocolates, darling.'

'The box has got your card in,' said Miss Bellever.

Alex peered down.

'So it has. How odd. How very odd . . . I certainly didn't send them.'

'What a very extraordinary thing,' said Miss Bellever.

'They look absolutely scrumptious,' said Gina, peering into the box. 'Look, Grandam, there are your favourite Kirsch ones in the middle.'

Miss Marple gently but firmly took the box away from her. Without a word she took it out of the room and went to find Lewis Serrocold. It took her some time because he had gone over to the College – she found him in Dr Maverick's room there. She put the box on the table in front of him. He listened to her brief account of the circumstances. His face grew suddenly stern and hard.

Carefully, he and the doctor lifted out chocolate after chocolate and examined them.

'I think,' said Dr Maverick, 'that these ones I have put aside have almost certainly been tampered with. You see the unevenness of the chocolate coating underneath? The next thing to do is to get them analysed.'

'But it seems incredible,' said Miss Marple. 'Why, everyone in the house might have been poisoned!'

Lewis nodded. His face was still white and hard.

'Yes. There is a ruthlessness – a disregard –' he broke off. 'Actually I think all these particular chocolates are Kirsch flavouring. That is Caroline's favourite. So, you see, there is knowledge behind this.'

Miss Marple said quietly:

'If it is as you suspect – if there is – *poison* – in these chocolates, then I'm afraid Carrie Louise will have to know what is going on. She must be put upon her guard.'

Lewis Serrocold said heavily:

'Yes. She will have to know that someone wants to kill her. I think that she will find it almost impossible to believe.'

Chapter 16

I

''Ere, Miss. Is it true as there's an 'ideous poisoner at work?'

Gina pushed the hair back from her forehead and jumped as the hoarse whisper reached her. There was paint on her cheek and paint on her slacks. She and her selected helpers had been busy on the backcloth of the Nile at Sunset for their next theatrical production.

It was one of these helpers who was now asking the question. Ernie, the boy who had given her such valuable lessons in the manipulation of locks. Ernie's fingers were equally dexterous at stage carpentry, and he was one of the most enthusiastic theatrical assistants.

His eyes now were bright and beady with pleasurable anticipation.

Ernie shut one eye.

'It's all round the dorms,' he said. 'But look 'ere,

Miss, it wasn't one of *us*. Not a thing like that. And nobody wouldn't do a thing to Mrs Serrocold. Even Jenkins wouldn't cosh *her*. 'Tisn't as though it was the old bitch. Wouldn't 'alf like to poison 'er, I wouldn't.'

'Don't talk like that about Miss Bellever.'

'Sorry, Miss. It slipped out. What poison was it, Miss? Strickline, was it? Makes you arch your back and die in agonies, that does. Or was it Prussian acid?'

'I don't know what you're talking about, Ernie.'

Ernie winked again.

'Not 'alf you don't! Mr Alex it was done it, so they say. Brought them chocs down from London. But that's a lie. Mr Alex wouldn't do a thing like that, would he, Miss?'

'Of course he wouldn't,' said Gina.

'Much more likely to be Mr Baumgarten. When he's giving us P.T. he makes the most awful faces, and Don and I think as he's batty.'

'Just move that turpentine out of the way.'

Ernie obeyed, murmuring to himself:

'Don't 'arf see life 'ere! Old Gulbrandsen done in yesterday and now a secret poisoner. D'you think it's the same person doing both? What 'ud you say, Miss, if I told you as I know oo it was done 'im in?'

'You can't possibly know anything about it.'

'Coo, carn't I neither? Supposin' I was outside last night and saw something.'

'How could you have been out? The College is locked up after roll call at seven.'

'Roll call . . . I can get out whenever I likes, Miss. Locks don't mean nothing to me. Get out and walk around the grounds just for the fun of it, I do.'

Gina said:

'I wish you'd stop telling lies, Ernie.'

'Who's telling lies?'

'You are. You tell lies and you boast about things that you've never done at all.'

'That's what you say, Miss. You wait till the coppers come round and arsk me all about what I saw last night.'

'Well, what did you see?'

'Ah,' said Ernie, 'wouldn't you like to know?'

Gina made a rush at him and he beat a strategic retreat. Stephen came over from the other side of the theatre and joined Gina. They discussed various technical matters and then, side by side, they walked back towards the house.

'They all seem to know about Grandam and the chocs,' said Gina. 'The boys, I mean. How do they get to know?'

'Local grapevine of some kind.'

'And they knew about Alex's card. Stephen, surely

Agatha Christie

it was very stupid to put Alex's card in the box when he was actually coming down here.'

'Yes, but who knew he was coming down here? He decided to come on the spur of the moment and sent a telegram. Probably the box was posted by then. And if he hadn't come down, putting his card in would have been quite a good idea. Because he does send Caroline chocolates sometimes.'

He went on slowly:

'What I simply can't understand is –'

'Is why anyone should want to poison, Grandam,' Gina cut in. 'I know. It's *inconceivable*! She's so adorable – and absolutely everyone *does* adore her.'

Stephen did not answer. Gina looked at him sharply.

'I know what you're thinking, Steve!'

'I wonder.'

'You're thinking that Wally – doesn't adore her. But Wally would never poison anyone. The idea's laughable.'

'The loyal wife!'

'Don't say that in that sneering tone of voice.'

'I didn't mean to sneer. I think you *are* loyal. I admire you for it. But darling Gina, you can't keep it up, you know.'

'What do you mean, Steve?'

'You know quite well what I mean. You and Wally

don't belong together. It's just one of those things that doesn't work. He knows it too. The split is going to come any day now. And you'll both be much happier when it has come.'

Gina said:

'Don't be idiotic.'

Stephen laughed.

'Come now, you can't pretend that you're suited to each other or that Wally's happy here.'

'Oh, I don't know what's the matter with him,' cried Gina. 'He sulks the whole time. He hardly speaks. I – I don't know what to do about him. Why can't he enjoy himself here? We had such fun together once – everything was fun – and now he might be a different person. Why do people have to change so?'

'Do I change?'

'No, Steve darling. You're always Steve. Do you remember how I used to tag round after you in the holidays?'

'And what a nuisance I used to think you – that miserable little kid Gina. Well, the tables are turned now. You've got me where you want me, haven't you, Gina?'

Gina said quickly:

'Idiot.' She went on hurriedly, 'Do you think Ernie was lying? He was pretending he was roaming about

229

in the fog last night, and hinting that he could tell things about the murder. Do you think that might be true?'

'True? Of course not. You know how he boasts. Anything to make himself important.'

'Oh, I know. I only wondered –'

They walked along side by side without speaking.

II

The setting sun illumined the west façade of the house. Inspector Curry looked towards it.

'Is this about the place where you stopped your car last night?' he asked.

Alex Restarick stood back a little as though considering.

'Near enough,' he said. 'It's difficult to tell exactly because of the fog. Yes, I should say this was the place.'

Inspector Curry stood looking round with an appraising eye.

The gravelled sweep of drive swept round in a slow curve, and at this point, emerging from a screen of rhododendrons, the west façade of the house came suddenly into view with its terrace and yew hedges and steps leading down to the lawns. Thereafter the drive continued in its curving progress, sweeping through a belt of trees and round between the lake and the house until it ended in the big gravel sweep at the east side of the house.

'Dodgett,' said Inspector Curry.

Police Constable Dodgett, who had been holding himself at the ready, started spasmodically into motion. He hurled himself across the intervening space of lawn in a diagonal line towards the house, reached the terrace, went in by the side door. A few moments later the curtains of one of the windows were violently agitated. Then Constable Dodgett reappeared out of the garden door, and ran back to rejoin them, breathing like a steam engine.

'Two minutes and forty-two seconds,' said Inspector Curry, clicking the stop watch with which he had been timing him. 'They don't take long, these things, do they?'

His tone was pleasantly conversational.

'I don't run as fast as your constable,' said Alex. 'I presume it *is* my supposed movements you have been timing?'

'I'm just pointing out that you had the opportunity to do murder. That's all, Mr Restarick. I'm not making any accusations – as yet.'

Alex Restarick said kindly to Constable Dodgett, who was still panting:

'I can't run as fast as you can, but I believe I'm in better training.'

'It's since 'aving the bronchitis last winter,' said Dodgett.

Alex turned back to the Inspector.

'Seriously, though, in spite of trying to make me uncomfortable and observing my reactions – and you must remember that we artistic folk are oh! so sensitive, such tender plants!' – his voice took on a mocking note – 'you can't really believe I had anything to do with all this? I'd hardly send a box of poisoned chocolates to Mrs Serrocold and put my card inside, would I?'

'That might be what we are meant to think. There's such a thing as a double bluff, Mr Restarick.'

'Oh, I see. How ingenious you are. By the way, those chocolates *were* poisoned?'

'The six chocolates containing Kirsch flavouring in the top layer were poisoned, yes. They contained aconitine.'

'Not one of my favourite poisons, Inspector. Personally, I have a weakness for curare.'

'Curare has to be introduced into the bloodstream, Mr Restarick, not into the stomach.'

'How wonderfully knowledgeable the police force are,' said Alex admiringly.

Inspector Curry cast a quiet sideways glance at the young man. He noted the slightly pointed ears, the un-English Mongolian type of face. The eyes that danced with mischievous mockery. It would have been hard at any time to know what Alex Restarick was thinking. A satyr – or did he mean a faun? An overfed faun, Inspector Curry thought suddenly, and somehow there was an unpleasantness about that idea.

A twister with brains – that's how he would sum up Alex Restarick. Cleverer than his brother. Mother had been a Russian or so he had heard. 'Russians' to Inspector Curry were what 'Bony' had been in the early days of the nineteenth century, and what 'the Huns' had been in the early twentieth century. Anything to do with Russia was bad in Inspector Curry's opinion, and if Alex Restarick had murdered Gulbrandsen he would be a very satisfactory criminal. But unfortunately Curry was by no means convinced that he had.

Constable Dodgett, having recovered his breath, now spoke.

'I moved the curtains as you told me, sir,' he said. 'And counted thirty. I noticed that the curtains have a hook torn off at the top. Means that there's a gap. You'd see the light in the room from outside.'

Inspector Curry said to Alex:

'Did you notice light streaming out from that window last night?'

'I couldn't see the house at all because of the fog. I told you so.'

233

'Fog's patchy, though. Sometimes it clears for a minute here and there.'

'It never cleared so that I could see the house – the main part, that is. The gymnasium building close at hand loomed up out of the mist in a deliciously unsubstantial way. It gave a perfect illusion of dock warehouses. As I told you, I am putting on a Limehouse Ballet and –'

'You told me,' agreed Inspector Curry.

'One gets in the habit, you know, of looking at things from the point of view of a stage set, rather than from the point of view of reality.'

'I daresay. And yet a stage set's real enough, isn't it, Mr Restarick?'

'I don't see exactly what you mean, Inspector.'

'Well, it's made of real materials – canvas and wood and paint and cardboard. The illusion is in the eye of the beholder, not in the set itself. That, as I say, is real enough, as real behind the scenes as it is in front.'

Alex stared at him.

'Now that, you know, is a *very* penetrating remark, Inspector. It's given me an idea.'

'For another ballet?'

'No, not for another ballet . . . Dear me, I wonder if we've all been rather stupid?'

III

The Inspector and Dodgett went back to the house across the lawn. (Looking for footprints, Alex said to himself. But here he was wrong. They had looked for footprints very early that morning and had been unsuccessful because it had rained heavily at 2 a.m.) Alex walked slowly up the drive, turning over in his mind the possibilities of his new idea.

He was diverted from this, however, by the sight of Gina walking on the path by the lake. The house was on a slight eminence, and the ground sloped gently down from the front sweeps of gravel to the lake, which was bordered by rhododendrons and other shrubs. Alex ran down the gravel and found Gina.

'If you could black out that absurd Victorian monstrosity,' he said, screwing up his eyes, 'this would make a very good Swan Lake, with you, Gina, as the Swan Maiden. You are more like the Snow Queen though, when I come to think of it. Ruthless, determined to have your own way, quite without pity or kindliness or the rudiments of compassion. You are very, *very* feminine, Gina dear.'

'How malicious you are, Alex dear!'

'Because I refuse to be taken in by you? You're very pleased with yourself, aren't you, Gina? You've got us all where you want us. Myself, Stephen, and that large simple husband of yours.'

'You're talking nonsense.'

'Oh no, I'm not. Stephen's in love with you. I'm in love with you, and Wally's desperately miserable. What more could a woman want?'

Gina looked at him and laughed.

Alex nodded his head vigorously.

'You have the rudiments of honesty, I'm glad to see. That's the Latin in you. You don't go to the trouble of pretending that you're not attractive to men – and that you're terribly sorry about it if they are attracted to you. You like having men in love with you, don't you, cruel Gina? Even miserable little Edgar Lawson!'

Gina looked at him steadily.

She said in a quiet serious tone:

'It doesn't last very long, you know. Women have a much worse time of it in the world than men do. They're more vulnerable. They have children, and they mind – terribly – about their children. As soon as they lose their looks, the men they love don't love them any more. They're betrayed and deserted and pushed aside. I don't blame men. I'd be the same myself. I don't like people who are old or ugly or ill or who whine about their troubles or who are ridiculous like Edgar, strutting about and pretending he's important and worthwhile. You say I'm cruel? It's a cruel world! Sooner or later it will be cruel to *me*! But now I'm young and I'm nice looking and people find me attractive.' Her teeth flashed out in her peculiar warm sunny smile. 'Yes, I enjoy it, Alex. Why shouldn't I?'

'Why indeed?' said Alex. 'What I want to know is what are you going to do about it. Are you going to marry Stephen or are you going to marry me?'

'I'm married to Wally.'

'Temporarily. Every woman should make one mistake matrimonially – but there's no need to dwell on it. Having tried out the show in the provinces, the time has come to bring it to the West End.'

'And you're the West End?'

'Indubitably.'

'Do you really want to marry me? I can't imagine you married.'

'I insist on marriage. *Affaires*, I always think, are so very old-fashioned. Difficulties with passports and hotels and all that. I shall *never* have a mistress unless I can't get her any other way!'

Gina's laugh rang out fresh and clear.

'You do amuse me, Alex.'

'It is my principal asset. Stephen is much better looking than I am. He's extremely handsome and very intense which, of course, women adore. But intensity is fatiguing in the home. With me, Gina, you will find life entertaining.'

'Aren't you going to say you love me madly?'

'However true that may be, I shall certainly not say it. It would be one up to you and one down to me if I did. No, all I am prepared to do is to make you a businesslike offer of marriage.'

'I shall have to think about it,' said Gina smiling.

'Naturally. Besides, you've got to put Wally out of his misery first. I've a lot of sympathy with Wally. It must be absolute hell for him to be married to you and trailed along at your chariot wheels into this heavy family atmosphere of philanthropy.'

'What a beast you are, Alex!'

'A perceptive beast.'

'Sometimes,' said Gina, 'I don't think Wally cares for me one little bit. He just doesn't notice me any more.'

'You've stirred him up with a stick and he doesn't respond? Most annoying.'

Like a flash Gina swung her palm and delivered a ringing slap on Alex's smooth cheek.

'Touché!' cried Alex.

With a quick deft movement he gathered her into his arms and before she could resist, his lips fastened on hers in a long ardent kiss. She struggled a moment and then relaxed . . .

'Gina!'

They sprang apart. Mildred Strete, her face red, her lips quivering, glared at them balefully. For a moment the eagerness of her words choked their utterance.

'Disgusting . . . disgusting . . . you abandoned beastly girl . . . you're just like your mother . . . You're a bad lot . . . I always knew you were a bad lot . . . utterly depraved . . . and you're not only an adulteress – you're a murderess too. Oh yes, you are. I know what I know!'

'And what do you know? Don't be ridiculous, Aunt Mildred.'

'I'm no aunt of yours, thank goodness. No blood relation to you. Why, you don't even know who your mother was or where she came from! But you know well enough what my father was like and my mother. What sort of a child do you think they would adopt? A criminal's child or prostitute's probably! That's the sort of people they were. They ought to have remembered that bad blood will tell. Though I daresay that it's the Italian in you that makes you turn to *poison*.'

'How dare you say that?'

'I shall say what I like. You can't deny now, can you, that somebody tried to poison mother? And who's the most likely person to do that? Who comes into an enormous fortune if mother dies? You do, Gina, and you may be sure that the police have not overlooked that fact.'

Still trembling, Mildred moved rapidly away.

'Pathological,' said Alex. 'Definitely pathological. Really *most* interesting. It makes one wonder about the late Canon Strete . . . religious scruples, perhaps? . . . Or would you say impotent?'

'Don't be disgusting, Alex. Oh I hate her, I hate her, I hate her.'

Gina clenched her hands and shook with fury.

'Lucky you hadn't got a knife in your stocking,' said Alex. 'If you had, dear Mrs Strete might have known something about murder from the point of view of the victim. Calm down, Gina. Don't look so melodramatic and like Italian Opera.'

'How dare she say I tried to poison Grandam?'

'Well, darling, *somebody* tried to poison her. And from the point of view of motive you're well in the picture, aren't you?'

'Alex!' Gina stared at him, dismayed. 'Do the police think so?'

'It's extremely difficult to know what the police think. . . . They keep their own counsel remarkably well. They're by no means fools, you know. That reminds me –'

'Where are you going?'

'To work out an idea of mine.'

Chapter 17

I

'You say somebody has been trying to *poison* me?'

Carrie Louise's voice held bewilderment and disbelief.

'You know,' she said, 'I can't really believe it . . .'

She waited a few moments, her eyes half closed.

Lewis said gently, 'I wish I could have spared you this, dearest.'

Almost absently she stretched out a hand to him and he took it.

Miss Marple, sitting close by, shook her head sympathetically.

Carrie Louise opened her eyes.

'Is it really true, Jane?' she asked.

'I'm afraid so, my dear.'

'Then everything –' Carrie Louise broke off.

She went on:

'I've always thought I knew what was real and what

wasn't . . . *This* doesn't seem real – but it is . . . So I may be wrong everywhere . . . But who could want to do such a thing to me? Nobody in this house could want to – *kill* me?'

Her voice still held incredulity.

'That's what I would have thought,' said Lewis. 'I was wrong.'

'And Christian knew about it? That explains it.'

'Explains what?' asked Lewis.

'His manner,' said Carrie Louise. 'It was very odd, you know. Not at all his usual self. He seemed – upset about me – as though he was wanting to say something to me – and then not saying it. And he asked me if my heart was strong? And if I'd been well lately? Trying to hint to me, perhaps. But why not say something straight out? It's so much simpler just to say it straight out.'

'He didn't want to – cause you pain, Caroline.'

'Pain? But why – Oh I see . . .' Her eyes widened. 'So *that's* what you believe. But you're wrong, Lewis, quite wrong. I can assure you of that.'

Her husband avoided her eyes.

'I'm sorry,' said Mrs Serrocold after a moment or two. 'But I can't believe anything of what has happened lately is true. Edgar shooting at you. Gina and Stephen. That ridiculous box of chocolates. It just isn't *true*.'

Nobody spoke.

Caroline Louise Serrocold sighed.

'I suppose,' she said, 'that I must have lived outside reality for a long time . . . Please, both of you, I think I would like to be alone . . . I've got to try and understand . . .'

II

Miss Marple came down the stairs and into the Great Hall to find Alex Restarick standing near the large arched entrance door with his hand flung out in a somewhat flamboyant gesture.

'Come in, come in,' said Alex happily and as though he were the owner of the Great Hall. 'I'm just thinking about last night.'

Lewis Serrocold, who had followed Miss Marple down from Carrie Louise's sitting-room, crossed the Great Hall to his study and went in and shut the door.

'Are you trying to reconstruct the crime?' asked Miss Marple with subdued eagerness.

'Eh?' Alex looked at her with a frown. Then his brow cleared.

'Oh *that*,' he said. 'No, not exactly. I was looking at the whole thing from an entirely different point of view. I was thinking of this place in the terms of the

243

theatre. Not reality, but artificiality! Just come over here. Think of it in the terms of a stage set. Lighting, entrances, exits. Dramatis Personae. Noises off. All very interesting. Not all my own idea. The Inspector gave it to me. I think he's rather a cruel man. He did his best to frighten me this morning.'

'And did he frighten you?'

'I'm not sure.'

Alex described the Inspector's experiment and the timing of the performance of the puffing Constable Dodgett.

'Time,' he said, 'is so very misleading. One thinks things take such a long time, but really, of course, they don't.'

'No,' said Miss Marple.

Representing the audience, she moved to a different position. The stage set now consisted of a vast tapestry covered wall going up to dimness, with a grand piano up L. and a window and window seat up R. Very near the window seat was the door into the library. The piano stool was only about eight feet from the door into the square lobby which led to the corridor. Two very convenient exits! The audience, of course, had an excellent view of both of them . . .

But last night, there had been no audience. Nobody, that is to say, had been facing the stage set that Miss Marple was now facing. The audience, last night, had been sitting with their backs to that particular stage.

How long, Miss Marple wondered, would it have taken to slip out of the room, run along the corridor, shoot Gulbrandsen and come back? Not nearly so long as one would think. Measured in minutes and seconds a very short time indeed . . .

What had Carrie Louise meant when she had said to her husband: 'So *that's* what you believe – but you're wrong, Lewis!'

'I must say that that was a very penetrating remark of the Inspector's,' Alex's voice cut in on her meditations. 'About a stage set being real. Made of wood and cardboard and stuck together with glue and as real on the unpainted as on the painted side. "The illusion," he pointed out, "is in the eyes of the audience."'

'Like conjurers,' Miss Marple murmured vaguely. '*They do it with mirrors* is, I believe, the slang phrase.'

Stephen Restarick came in, slightly out of breath.

'Hallo, Alex,' he said. 'That little rat, Ernie Gregg – I don't know if you remember him?'

'The one who played Feste when you did Twelfth Night? Quite a bit of talent there, I thought.'

'Yes, he's got talent of a sort. Very good with his hands too. Does a lot of our carpentry. However, that's neither here nor there. He's been boasting to Gina that he gets out at night and wanders about the grounds.

Says he was wandering round last night and boasts he saw something.'

Alex spun round.

'Saw what?'

'Says he's not going to tell. Actually I'm pretty certain he's only trying to show off and get into the limelight. He's an awful liar, but I thought perhaps he ought to be questioned.'

Alex said sharply: 'I should leave him for a bit. Don't let him think we're too interested.'

'Perhaps – yes, I think you may be right there. This evening, perhaps.'

Stephen went on into the library.

Miss Marple, moving gently round the Hall in her character of mobile audience, collided with Alex Restarick as he stepped back suddenly.

Miss Marple said, 'I'm so sorry.'

Alex frowned at her, said in an absent sort of way:

'I beg your pardon,' and then added in a surprised voice: 'Oh, it's *you*.'

It seemed to Miss Marple an odd remark for someone with whom she had been conversing for some considerable time.

'I was thinking of something else,' said Alex Restarick. 'That boy Ernie –' He made vague motions with both hands.

Then, with a sudden change of manner, he crossed

the Hall and went through the library door, shutting it behind him.

The murmur of voices came from behind the closed door, but Miss Marple hardly noticed them. She was uninterested in the versatile Ernie and what he had seen or pretended to see. She had a shrewd suspicion that Ernie had seen nothing at all. She did not believe for a moment that on a cold raw foggy night like last night, Ernie would have troubled to use his lockpicking activities and wander about in the Park. In all probability he never had got out at night. Boasting, that was all it had been.

'Like Johnnie Backhouse,' thought Miss Marple, who always had a good storehouse of parallels to draw upon selected from inhabitants of St Mary Mead.

'I seen you last night,' had been Johnnie Backhouse's unpleasant taunt to all he thought it might affect.

It had been a surprisingly successful remark. So many people, Miss Marple reflected, have been in places where they are anxious not to be seen!

She dismissed Johnnie from her mind and concentrated on a vague something which Alex's account of Inspector Curry's remarks had stirred to life. Those remarks had given Alex an idea. She was not sure that they had not given her an idea, too. The same idea? Or a different one?

She stood where Alex Restarick had stood. She

thought to herself, 'This is not a real Hall. This is only cardboard and canvas and wood. This is a stage scene . . .' Scrappy phrases flashed across her mind. 'Illusion –' 'In the eyes of the audience.' '*They do it with mirrors* . . .' Bowls of goldfish . . . yards of coloured ribbon . . . vanishing ladies . . . all the panoply and misdirection of the conjurer's art . . .

Something stirred in her consciousness – a picture – something that Alex had said . . . something that he had described to her . . . Constable Dodgett puffing and panting . . . Panting . . . Something shifted in her mind – came into sudden focus . . .

'Why of *course*!' said Miss Marple. 'That must be it . . .'

Chapter 18

I

'Oh, Wally, how you startled me!'

Gina, emerging from the shadows by the theatre, jumped back a little, as the figure of Wally Hudd materialized out of the gloom. It was not yet quite dark, but had that eerie half light when objects lose their reality and take on the fantastic shapes of nightmare.

'What are you doing down here? You never come near the theatre as a rule.'

'Maybe I was looking for you, Gina. It's usually the best place to find you, isn't it?'

Wally's soft, faintly drawling voice held no special insinuation, and yet Gina flinched a little.

'It's a job and I'm keen on it. I like the atmosphere of paint and canvas, and back stage generally.'

'Yes. It means a lot to you. I've seen that. Tell me, Gina, how long do you think it will be before this business is all cleared up?'

'The inquest's tomorrow. It will just be adjourned for a fortnight or something like that. At least, that's what Inspector Curry gave us to understand.'

'A fortnight,' said Wally thoughtfully. 'I see. Say three weeks, perhaps. And after that – we're free. I'm going back to the States then.'

'Oh! but I can't rush off like that,' cried Gina. 'I couldn't leave Grandam. And we've got these two new productions we're working on –'

'I didn't say "*we*." I said *I* was going.'

Gina stopped and looked up at her husband. Something in the effect of the shadows made him seem very big. A big, quiet figure – and in some way, or so it seemed to her, faintly menacing . . . Standing over her. Threatening – what?

'Do you mean' – she hesitated – 'you don't want me to come?'

'Why, no – I didn't say that.'

'You don't care if I come or not? Is that it?'

She was suddenly angry.

'See here, Gina. This is where we've got to have a showdown. We didn't know much about each other when we got married – not much about each other's backgrounds, not much about the other one's folks. We thought it didn't matter. We thought nothing mattered except having a swell time together. Well, stage one is over. Your folks didn't – and don't – think much of me. Maybe they're right. I'm not their kind. But if you think I'm staying on here, kicking my heels, and doing odd jobs in what I consider is just a crazy set-up – well, think again! I want to live in my own country, doing the kind of job I want to do, and can do. My idea of a wife is the kind of wife who used to go along with the old pioneers, ready for anything, hardship, unfamiliar country, danger, strange surroundings . . . Perhaps that's too much to ask of you, but it's that or nothing! Maybe I hustled you into marriage. If so, you'd better get free of me and start again. It's up to you. If you prefer one of these arty boys – it's your life and you've got to choose. But I'm going home.'

'I think you're an absolute *pig*,' said Gina. 'I'm enjoying myself here.'

'Is that so? Well, I'm not. You even enjoy murder, I suppose?'

Gina drew in her breath sharply.

'That's a cruel wicked thing to say. I was very fond of Uncle Christian. And don't you realize that someone has been quietly poisoning Grandam for months? It's horrible!'

'I told you I didn't like it here. I don't like the kind of things that go on. I'm quitting.'

'If you're allowed to! Don't you realize you'll probably be arrested for Uncle Christian's murder? I hate the way Inspector Curry looks at you. He's just like a cat watching a mouse with a nasty sharp-clawed paw all ready to pounce. Just because you were out of the Hall fixing those lights, and because you're not English, I'm sure they'll go fastening it on you.'

'They'll need some evidence first.'

Gina wailed:

'I'm frightened for you, Wally. I've been frightened all along.'

'No good being scared. I tell you they've got nothing on me!'

They walked in silence towards the house.

Gina said:

'I don't believe you really want me to come back to America with you . . .'

Walter Hudd did not answer.

Gina Hudd turned on him and stamped her foot.

'I hate you. I hate you. You are horrible – a beast – a cruel unfeeling beast. After all I've tried to do for you! You want to be rid of me. You don't care if you never see me again. Well, I don't care if *I* never see *you* again! I was a stupid little fool ever to marry you, and I shall get a divorce as soon as possible, and I shall marry Stephen or Alexis and be much happier than I ever could be with you. And I hope you go back to the States and marry some horrible girl who makes you really miserable!'

'Fine!' said Wally. 'Now we know where we are!'

II

Miss Marple saw Gina and Wally go into the house together.

She was standing at the spot where Inspector Curry had made his experiment with Constable Dodgett earlier in the afternoon.

Miss Bellever's voice behind her made her jump.

'You'll get a chill, Miss Marple, standing about like that after the sun's gone down.'

Miss Marple fell meekly into step with her and they walked briskly through the house.

'I was thinking about conjuring tricks,' said Miss Marple. 'So difficult when you're watching them to see how they're done, and yet, once they are explained, so absurdly simple. (Although, even now, I can't imagine how conjurers produce bowls of goldfish!) Did you ever see the Lady who is Sawn in Half – *such* a thrilling trick. It fascinated me when I was eleven years old, I remember. And I never *could* think how it was done. But the other day there was an article in some paper giving the whole thing away. I don't think a newspaper should do that, do you? It seems it's not one girl – but *two*. The head of one and the feet of the other. You think it's one girl and it's really two – and the other way round would work equally well, wouldn't it?'

Agatha Christie

Miss Bellever looked at her with faint surprise.

Miss Marple was not often so fluffy and incoherent as this. 'It's all been too much for the old lady,' she thought.

'When you only look at one side of a thing, you only see one side,' continued Miss Marple. 'But everything fits in perfectly well if you can only make up your mind what is reality and what is illusion.' She added abruptly, 'Is Carrie Louise – all right?'

'Yes,' said Miss Bellever. 'She's all right, but it must have been a shock, you know – finding out that someone wanted to kill her. I mean particularly a shock to her, because she doesn't understand violence.'

'Carrie Louise understands some things that we don't,' said Miss Marple thoughtfully. 'She always has.'

'I know what you mean – but she doesn't live in the real world.'

'Doesn't she?'

Miss Bellever looked at her in surprise.

'There never was a more unworldly person than Cara –'

'You don't think that perhaps –' Miss Marple broke off, as Edgar Lawson passed them, swinging along at a great pace. He gave a kind of shamefaced nod, but averted his face as he passed.

'I've remembered now who he reminds me of,' said

Miss Marple. 'It came to me suddenly just a few moments ago. He reminds me of a young man called Leonard Wylie. His father was a dentist, but he got old and blind and his hand used to shake, and so people preferred to go to the son. But the old man was very miserable about it, and moped, said he was no good for anything any more, and Leonard who was very soft-hearted and rather foolish, began to pretend he drank more than he should. He always smelt of whisky and he used to sham being rather fuddled when his patients came. His idea was that they'd go back to the father again and say the younger man was no good.'

'And did they?'

'Of course not,' said Miss Marple. 'What happened was what anybody with any sense could have told him would happen! The patients went to Mr Reilly, the rival dentist. So many people with good hearts have no sense. Besides, Leonard Wylie was so unconvincing . . . His idea of drunkenness wasn't in the least like real drunkenness, and he overdid the whisky – spilling it on his clothes, you know, to a perfectly impossible extent.'

They went into the house by the side door.

Chapter 19

I

Inside the house, they found the family assembled in the library. Lewis was walking up and down, and there was an air of general tension in the atmosphere.

'Is anything the matter?' asked Miss Bellever.

Lewis said shortly: 'Ernie Gregg is missing from roll call tonight.'

'Has he run away?'

'We don't know. Maverick and some of the staff are searching the grounds. If we cannot find him we must communicate with the police.'

'Grandam!' Gina ran over to Carrie Louise, startled by the whiteness of her face. 'You look ill.'

'I am unhappy. The poor boy . . .'

Lewis said: 'I was going to question him this evening as to whether he had seen anything noteworthy last night. I have the offer of a good post for him and I thought that after discussing that, I would bring up the other topic. Now –' he broke off.

Miss Marple murmured softly:

'Foolish boy . . . Poor foolish boy . . .'

She shook her head, and Mrs Serrocold said gently: 'So *you* think so too, Jane . . . ?'

Stephen Restarick came in. He said, 'I missed you at the theatre, Gina. I thought you said you would – Hallo, what's up?'

Lewis repeated his information, and as he finished speaking, Dr Maverick came in with a fair-haired boy with pink cheeks and a suspiciously angelic expression. Miss Marple remembered his being at dinner on the night she had arrived at Stonygates.

'I've brought Arthur Jenkins along,' said Dr Maverick. 'He seems to have been the last person to talk to Ernie.'

'Now, Arthur,' said Lewis Serrocold, 'please help us if you can. Where has Ernie gone? Is this just a prank?'

'I dunno, sir. Straight, I don't. Didn't say nothing to me, he didn't. All full of the play at the theatre he was, that's all. Said as how he'd had a smashing idea for the scenery, what Mrs Hudd and Mr Stephen thought was first class.'

'There's another thing, Arthur. Ernie claims he was prowling about the grounds after lock-up last night. Was that true?'

''Course it ain't. Just boasting, that's all. Perishing liar, Ernie. *He* never got out at night. Used to boast he could, but he wasn't that good with locks! He couldn't do anything with a lock as was a lock. Anyway 'e was in larst night, that I do know.'

'You're not saying that just to satisfy us, Arthur?'

'Cross my heart,' said Arthur virtuously.

Lewis did not look quite satisfied.

'Listen,' said Dr Maverick. 'What's that?'

A murmur of voices was approaching. The door was flung open and looking very pale and ill, the spectacled Mr Baumgarten staggered in.

He gasped out: 'We've found him – them. It's horrible . . .'

He sank down on a chair and mopped his forehead.

Mildred Strete said sharply:

'What do you mean – found *them*?'

Baumgarten was shaking all over.

'Down at the theatre,' he said. 'Their heads crushed in – the big counterweight must have fallen on them. Alexis Restarick and that boy Ernie Gregg. They're both dead . . .'

Chapter 20

I

'I've brought you a cup of strong soup, Carrie Louise,' said Miss Marple. 'Now please drink it.'

Mrs Serrocold sat up in the big carved oak four-poster bed. She looked very small and childlike. Her cheeks had lost their pink flush, and her eyes had a curiously absent look.

She took the soup obediently from Miss Marple. As she sipped it, Miss Marple sat down in a chair beside the bed.

'First, Christian,' said Carrie Louise, 'and now Alex – and poor, sharp, silly little Ernie. Did he really – know anything?'

'I don't think so,' said Miss Marple. 'He was just telling lies – making himself important by hinting that he had seen or knew something. The tragedy is that somebody believed his lies . . .'

Agatha Christie

Carrie Louise shivered. Her eyes went back to their far away look.

'We meant to do so much for these boys . . . We did do something. Some of them have done wonderfully well. Several of them are in really responsible positions. A few slid back – that can't be helped. Modern civilized conditions are so complex – too complex for some simple and undeveloped natures. You know Lewis's great scheme? He always felt that transportation was a thing that had saved many a potential criminal in the past. They were shipped overseas – and they made new lives in simpler surroundings. He wants to start a modern scheme on that basis. To buy up a great tract of territory – or a group of islands. Finance it for some years, make it a co-operative self-supporting community – with everyone taking a stake in it. But cut off so that the early temptation to go back to cities and the bad old days can be neutralized. It's his dream. But it will take a lot of money, of course, and there aren't many philanthropists with vision now. We want another Eric. Eric would have been enthusiastic.'

Miss Marple picked up a little pair of scissors and looked at them curiously.

'What an odd pair of scissors,' she said. 'They've got two fingers holes on one side and one on the other.'

Carrie Louise's eyes came back from that frightening far distance.

'Alex gave them to me this morning,' she said. 'They're supposed to make it easier to cut your right hand nails. Dear boy, he was so enthusiastic. He made me try them then and there.'

'And I suppose he gathered up the nail clippings and took them tidily away,' said Miss Marple.

'Yes,' said Carrie Louise. 'He –' She broke off. 'Why did you say that?'

'I was thinking about Alex. He had brains. Yes, he had brains.'

'You mean – that's why he died?'

'I think so – yes.'

'He and Ernie – it doesn't bear thinking about. When do they think it happened?'

'Late this evening. Between six and seven o'clock probably . . .'

'After they'd knocked off work for the day?'

'Yes.'

Gina had been down there that evening – and Wally Hudd. Stephen, too, said he had been down to look for Gina . . .

But as far as that went, anybody could have –

Miss Marple's train of thought was interrupted.

Carrie Louise said quietly and unexpectedly:

'How much do you know, Jane?'

Miss Marple looked up sharply. The eyes of the two women met.

Miss Marple said slowly: 'If I was quite sure . . .'

'I think you are sure, Jane.'

Jane Marple said slowly, 'What do you want me to do?'

Carrie leaned back against her pillows.

'It is in your hands, Jane – You'll do what you think right.'

She closed her eyes.

'Tomorrow' – Miss Marple hesitated – 'I shall have to try and talk to Inspector Curry – if he'll listen . . .'

Chapter 21

I

Inspector Curry said rather impatiently:

'Yes, Miss Marple?'

'Could we, do you think, go into the Great Hall.'

Inspector Curry looked faintly surprised.

'Is that your idea of privacy? Surely in here –'

He looked round the study.

'It's not privacy I'm thinking of so much. It's something I want to show you. Something Alex Restarick made me see.'

Inspector Curry, stifling a sigh, got up and followed Miss Marple.

'Somebody has been talking to you?' he suggested hopefully.

'No,' said Miss Marple. 'It's not a question of what people have said. It's really a question of conjuring tricks. They do it with mirrors, you know – that sort of thing – if you understand me.'

Agatha Christie

Inspector Curry did not understand. He stared and wondered if Miss Marple was quite right in the head.

Miss Marple took up her stand and beckoned the Inspector to stand beside her.

'I want you to think of this place as a stage set, Inspector. As it was on the night Christian Gulbrandsen was killed. You're here in the audience looking at the people on the stage. Mrs Serrocold and myself and Mrs Strete, and Gina and Stephen – and just like on the stage there are entrances and exits and the characters go out to different places. Only you don't think when you're in the audience where they are really going to. They go out "to the front door" or "to the kitchen" and when the door opens you see a little bit of painted backcloth. But *really* of course they go out to the wings – or the back of the stage with carpenters and electricians, and other characters waiting to come on – they go out – to a different world.'

'I don't quite see, Miss Marple –'

'Oh, I know – I daresay it sounds very silly – but if you think of this as a play and the scene is "the Great Hall at Stonygates" – what exactly is *behind* the scene? – I mean – what is back stage? The *terrace* – isn't it? – the terrace *and a lot of windows opening on to it*.

'And that, you see, is how the conjuring trick was done. It was the trick of the Lady Sawn in Half that made me think of it.'

'The Lady Sawn in Half?' Inspector Curry was now quite sure that Miss Marple was a mental case.

'A most thrilling conjuring trick. You must have seen it – only not really one girl but two girls. The head of one and the feet of the other. It looks like one person and is really two. And so I thought it could just as well be *the other way about. Two* people could be really one person.'

'Two people really one?' Inspector Curry looked desperate.

'Yes. Not for long. How long did your constable take in the Park to run to this house and back? Two minutes and forty-five seconds, wasn't it? This would be less than that. Well under two minutes.'

'What was under two minutes?'

'The conjuring trick. The trick when it wasn't two people but one person. In there – in the study. We're only looking at the visible part of the stage. Behind the scenes there is the terrace and a *row of windows*. So easy when there are two people in the study to open the study window, get out, run along the terrace (those footsteps Alex heard), in at the side door, shoot Christian Gulbrandsen and run back, and during that time, the other person in the study does both voices so that we're all quite sure there are *two* people in there. And so there were most of the time, but not for that little period of under two minutes.'

Inspector Curry found his breath and his voice.

'Do you mean that it was *Edgar Lawson* who ran along the terrace and shot Gulbrandsen? Edgar Lawson who poisoned Mrs Serrocold?'

'But you see, Inspector, *no one has been poisoning Mrs Serrocold at all.* That's where the misdirection comes in. Someone very cleverly used the fact that Mrs Serrocold's sufferings from arthritis were not unlike the symptoms of arsenical poisoning. It's the old conjurer's trick of forcing a card on you. Quite easy to add arsenic to a bottle of tonic – quite easy to add a few lines to a typewritten letter. But the *real* reason for Mr Gulbrandsen's coming here was the most likely reason – something to do with the Gulbrandsen Trust. Money, in fact. Suppose that there had been embezzlement – embezzlement on a very big scale – you see where that points? To just one person –'

Inspector Curry gasped: 'Lewis Serrocold?' he murmured incredulously.

'*Lewis Serrocold* . . .' said Miss Marple.

Chapter 22

I

Part of letter from Gina Hudd to her aunt Mrs Van Rydock:

– and so you see, darling Aunt Ruth, the whole thing has been just like a nightmare – especially the end of it. I've told you all about this funny man Edgar Lawson. He always was a complete rabbit – and when the Inspector began questioning him and breaking him down, he lost his nerve completely and scuttled like a rabbit. Just lost his nerve and ran – literally ran. Jumped out of the window and round the house and down the drive and then there was a policeman coming to head him off, and he swerved and ran full tilt for the lake. He leaped into a rotten old punt that's mouldered there for years and pushed off. Quite a mad senseless thing to do, of course, but as I say he was just a panic-stricken rabbit. And then Lewis gave a great shout and said 'That punt's rotten,' and raced off

269

*to the lake too. The punt went down and there was Edgar
struggling in the water. He couldn't swim. Lewis jumped
in and swam out to him. He got to him but they were both
in difficulty because they'd got among the reeds. One of
the Inspector's men went in with a rope round him but
he got entangled too and they had to pull him in. Aunt
Mildred said 'They'll drown – they'll drown – they'll both
drown . . .' in a silly sort of way, and Grandam just said
'Yes.' I can't describe to you just how she made that one
word sound. Just 'YES' and it went through you like –
like a sword.*

*Am I being just silly and melodramatic? I suppose I am.
But it did sound like that . . .*

*And then – when it was all over, and they'd got them
out and tried artificial respiration (but it was no good), the
Inspector came to us and said to Grandam: 'I'm afraid,
Mrs Serrocold, there's no hope.'*

Grandam said very quietly:

'Thank you, Inspector.'

*Then she looked at us all. Me longing to help but not
knowing how, and Jolly, looking grim and tender and
ready to minister as usual, and Stephen stretching out his
hands, and funny old Miss Marple looking so sad, and
tired, and even Wally looking upset. All so fond of her
and wanting to do SOMETHING.*

*But Grandam just said 'Mildred.' And Aunt Mildred
said 'Mother.' And they went away together into the*

house, Grandam looking so small and frail and leaning on Aunt Mildred. I never realized, until then, how fond of each other they were. It didn't show much, you know, but it was there all the time.

Gina paused and sucked the end of her fountain pen. She resumed:

About me and Wally – we're coming back to the States as soon as we can . . .

Chapter 23

I

'What made you guess, Jane?'

Miss Marple took her time about replying. She looked thoughtfully at the other two – Carrie Louise thinner and frailer and yet curiously untouched – and the old man with the sweet smile and the thick white hair. Dr Galbraith, Bishop of Cromer.

The Bishop took Carrie Louise's hand in his.

'This has been a great sorrow to you, my poor child, and a great shock.'

'A sorrow, yes, but not really a shock.'

'No,' said Miss Marple. 'That's what I discovered, you know. Everyone kept saying how Carrie Louise lived in another world from this and was out of touch with reality. But actually, Carrie Louise, it was reality you were in touch with, and not the illusion. You are never deceived by illusion like most of us are. When I suddenly realized that, I saw that I must go by what *you* thought and felt. You were quite sure that no one would try to poison you, you couldn't believe it – and you were quite right *not* to believe it, because it wasn't so! You never believed that Edgar would harm Lewis – and again you were right. He never *would* have harmed Lewis. You were sure that Gina did not love anyone but her husband – and that again was quite true.

'So therefore, if I was to go by you, all the things that *seemed* to be true were only illusions. Illusions created for a definite purpose – in the same way that conjurers create illusions, to deceive an audience. We were the audience.

'Alex Restarick got an inkling of the truth first because he had the chance of seeing things from a different angle – from the outside angle. He was with the Inspector in the drive, and he looked at the house and realized the possibilities of the windows – and he remembered the sound of running feet he had heard that night, and then the timing of the constable showed him what a very short time things take to what we should imagine they would take. The constable panted a lot, and later, thinking of a puffing constable, I remembered that Lewis Serrocold was out of breath that night when he opened the study door. He'd just been running hard, you see . . .

'But it was Edgar Lawson that was the pivot of it all to me. There was always something wrong to me about Edgar Lawson. All the things he said and did were exactly right for what he was supposed to be, but he himself wasn't right. Because he was actually a normal young man playing the part of a schizophrenic – and he was always, as it were, a little larger than life. He was always theatrical.

'It must have all been very carefully planned and thought out. Lewis must have realized on the occasion of Christian's last visit that something had aroused his suspicions. And he knew Christian well enough to know that if he suspected he would not rest until he had satisfied himself that his suspicions were either justified or unfounded.'

Carrie Louise stirred.

'Yes,' she said. 'Christian was like that. Slow and painstaking, but actually very shrewd. I don't know what it was aroused his suspicions but he started investigating – and he found out the truth.'

The Bishop said: 'I blame myself for not having been a more conscientious trustee.'

'It was never expected of you to understand finance,' said Carrie Louise. 'That was originally Mr Gilfoy's province. Then, when he died, Lewis's great experience put him in what amounted to complete control. And that, of course, was what went to his head.'

The pink colour came up in her cheeks.

'Lewis was a great man,' she said. 'A man of great

vision, and a passionate believer in what could be accomplished – with money. He didn't want it for himself – or at least not in the greedy vulgar sense – he did want the power of it – he wanted the power to do great good with it –'

'He wanted,' said the Bishop, 'to be God.' His voice was suddenly stern. 'He forgot that man is only the humble instrument of God's will.'

'And so he embezzled the Trust funds?' said Miss Marple.

Dr Galbraith hesitated.

'It wasn't only that . . .'

'Tell her,' said Carrie Louise. 'She is my oldest friend.'

The Bishop said:

'Lewis Serrocold was what one might call a financial wizard. In his years of highly technical accountancy, he had amused himself by working out various methods of swindling which were practically foolproof. This had been merely an academic study, but when he once began to envisage the possibilities that a vast sum of money could encompass, he put these methods into practice. You see, he had at his disposal some first-class material. Amongst the boys who passed through here, he chose out a small select band. They were boys whose bent was naturally criminal, who loved excitement and who had a very high order of intelligence. We've not got nearly to the bottom of it all, but it seems clear that this esoteric circle was secret and specially trained and were later placed in key positions, where, by carrying out Lewis's directions, books were falsified in such a way that large sums of money were converted without any suspicion being aroused. I gather that the operations and the ramifications are so complicated that it will be months before the auditors can unravel it all. But the net result seems to be that under various names and banking accounts and companies Lewis Serrocold would have been able to dispose of a colossal sum with which he intended to establish an overseas colony for a co-operative experiment in which juvenile delinquents should eventually own this territory and administer it. It may have been a fantastic dream –'

'It was a dream that might have come true,' said Carrie Louise.

'Yes, it might have come true. But the means Lewis Serrocold adopted were dishonest means, and Christian Gulbrandsen discovered that. He was very upset, particularly by the realization of what the discovery and the probable prosecution of Lewis would mean to you, Carrie Louise.'

'That's why he asked me if my heart was strong, and seemed so worried about my health,' said Carrie Louise. 'I couldn't understand it.'

'Then Lewis Serrocold arrived back from the North

and Christian met him outside the house and told him that he knew what was going on. Lewis took it calmly, I think. Both men agreed they must do all they could to spare you. Christian said he would write to me and ask me to come here, as a co-trustee, to discuss the position.'

'But of course,' said Miss Marple, 'Lewis Serrocold had already prepared for this emergency. It was all planned. He had brought the young man who was to play the part of Edgar Lawson to the house. There was a real Edgar Lawson – of course – in case the police looked up his record. This false Edgar knew exactly what he had to do – act the part of a schizophrenic victim of persecution – and give Lewis Serrocold an alibi for a few vital minutes.

'The next step had been thought out too. Lewis's story that you, Carrie Louise, were being slowly poisoned – when one actually came to think of it there was only Lewis's story of what Christian had told *him* – that, and a few lines added on the typewriter whilst he was waiting for the police. It was easy to add arsenic to the tonic. No danger for you there – since he was on the spot to prevent you drinking it. The chocolates were just an added touch – and of course the original chocolates weren't poisoned – only those he substituted before turning them over to Inspector Curry.'

'And Alex guessed,' said Carrie Louise.

'Yes – that's why he collected your nail parings. They would show if arsenic actually had been administered over a long period.'

'Poor Alex – poor Ernie.'

There was a moment's silence as the other two thought of Christian Gulbrandsen, of Alexis Restarick, and of the boy Ernie – and of how quickly the act of murder could distort and deform.

'But surely,' said the Bishop, 'Lewis was taking a big risk in persuading Edgar to be his accomplice – even if he had some hold over him –'

Carrie shook her head.

'It wasn't exactly a hold over him. Edgar was devoted to Lewis.'

'Yes,' said Miss Marple. 'Like Leonard Wylie and his father. I wonder perhaps if –'

She paused delicately.

'You saw the likeness, I suppose?' said Carrie Louise. 'So you knew that all along?'

'I guessed. I knew Lewis had once had a short infatuation for an actress, before he met me. He told me about it. It wasn't serious, she was a gold-digging type of woman and she didn't care for him, but I've no doubt at all that Edgar was actually Lewis's son . . .'

'Yes,' said Miss Marple. 'That explains everything . . .'

'And he gave his life for him in the end,' said Carrie

Louise. She looked pleadingly at the Bishop. 'He did, you know.'

There was a silence and then Carrie Louise said:

'I'm glad it ended that way . . . with his life given in the hope of saving the boy . . . People who can be very good can be very bad, too. I always knew that was true about Lewis . . . But – he loved me very much – and I loved him.'

'Did you – ever suspect him?' asked Miss Marple.

'No,' said Carrie Louise. 'Because I was puzzled by the poisoning. I knew Lewis would never poison me and yet that letter of Christian's said definitely that someone *was* poisoning me – so I thought that everything I thought I knew about people must be wrong . . .'

Miss Marple said: 'But when Alex and Ernie were found killed. You suspected then?'

'Yes,' said Carrie Louise. 'Because I didn't think anyone else but Lewis would have dared. And I began to be afraid of what he might do next . . .'

She shivered slightly.

'I admired Lewis. I admired his – what shall I call it – his goodness? But I do see that if you're – good, you have to be humble as well.'

Dr Galbraith said gently:

'That, Carrie Louise, is what I have always admired in you – your humility.'

The lovely blue eyes opened wide in surprise.

'But *I'm* not clever – and not particularly good. I can only admire goodness in other people.'

'Dear Carrie Louise,' said Miss Marple.

Epilogue

'I think Grandam will be quite all right with Aunt Mildred,' said Gina. 'Aunt Mildred seems much nicer now – not so peculiar, if you know what I mean?'

'I know what you mean,' said Miss Marple.

'So Wally and I will go back to the States in a fortnight's time.'

Gina cast a look sideways at her husband.

'I shall forget all about Stonygates and Italy and all my girlish past and become a hundred per cent American. Our son will be always addressed as Junior. I can't say fairer than that, can I, Wally?'

'You certainly cannot, Kate,' said Miss Marple.

Wally, smiling indulgently at an old lady who got names wrong, corrected her gently:

'Gina, not Kate.'

But Gina laughed.

'She knows what she's saying! You see – she'll call *you* Petruchio in a moment!'

'I just think,' said Miss Marple to Walter, 'that you have acted very wisely, my dear boy.'

'She thinks you're just the right husband for me,' said Gina.

Miss Marple looked from one to the other. It was very nice, she thought, to see two young people so much in love, and Walter Hudd was completely transformed from the sulky young man she had first encountered into a good-humoured smiling giant . . .

'You two remind me,' she said, 'of –'

Gina rushed forward and placed a hand firmly over Miss Marple's mouth.

'No, darling,' she exclaimed. 'Don't say it. I'm suspicious of these village parallels. They've always got a sting in the tail. You really are a wicked old woman, you know.'

Her eyes went misty.

'When I think of you, and Aunt Ruth and Grandam all being young together . . . How I wonder what you were all like! I can't imagine it somehow . . .'

'I don't suppose you can,' said Miss Marple. 'It was all a long time ago . . .'